HERBERT CARTER'S LEGACY

It is practical, I will pay one thousand dollars a year for ten years for a half interest in the invention.

HERBERT CARTER'S LEGACY

OR

THE INVENTOR'S SON

BY

HORATIO ALGER, Jr.

Author of
"A Cousin's Conspiracy," "Hector's Inheritance," "Paul the Peddler," "Risen from the Ranks"

Made in U. S. A.

M. A. DONOHUE & COMPANY
CHICAGO :: NEW YORK

HERBERT CARTER'S LEGACY

CHAPTER I

MRS. CARTER RECEIVES A LETTER

"Is that the latest style?" inquired James Leech, with a sneer, pointing to a patch on the knee of Herbert Carter's pants.

Herbert's face flushed. He was not ashamed of the patch, for he knew that his mother's poverty made it a necessity. But he felt that it was mean and dishonorable in James Leech, whose father was one of the rich men of Wrayburn, to taunt him with what he could not help. Some boys might have slunk away abashed, but Herbert had pluck and stood his ground.

"It is my style," he answered, firmly, looking James boldly in the face.

"I admire your taste, then," returned James, with a smooth sneer.

"Then, you had better imitate it," retorted Herbert.

"Thank you," said James, in the same insulting tone. "Would you lend me your pants for a pattern? Excuse me, though; perhaps you have no other pair."

"For shame, James!" exclaimed one or two boys who had listened to the colloquy, stirred to indignation by this heartless insult on the part of James Leech to a boy who was deservedly a favorite with them all.

Herbert's fist involuntarily doubled, and James, though he did not know it, ran a narrow chance of getting a good whipping. But our young hero controlled himself, not without some difficulty, and said: "I have one other pair, and these are at your service whenever you require them."

Then turning to the other boys, he said, in a changed tone: "Who's in for a game of ball?"

"I," said one, promptly.

"And I," said another.

Herbert walked away, accompanied by the other boys, leaving James Leech alone.

James looked after him with a scowl. He was sharp enough to see that Herbert, in spite of his patched pants, was a better scholar and a greater favorite than himself. He had intended to humiliate him on the present occasion, but he was forced to acknowledge that he had come off second best from the encounter. He walked moodily away, and took what comfort he could in the thought that he was far superior to a boy who owned but two pairs of pants, and one of them patched. He was foolish enough to feel that a boy or man derived importance from the extent of his wardrobe; and exulted in the personal possession of eight pairs of pants.

This scene occurred at recess.

After school was over, Herbert walked home. He was a little thoughtful. There was no disgrace in a patch, as he was sensible enough to be aware. Still, he would have a little preferred not to wear one. That was only natural. In that point, I suppose, my readers will fully agree with him. But he knew very well that his mother, who had been left a widow, had hard work enough to get along as it was, and he had no idea of troubling her on the subject. Besides, he had a better suit for Sundays, neat though plain, and he felt that he ought not to be disturbed by James Leech's insolence.

So thinking, he neared the small house which he called home. It was a small cottage, with something less than an acre of land attached, enough upon which to raise a few vegetables. It belonged to his mother, nominally, but was mortgaged for half its value to Squire Leech, the father of James. The amount of the mortgage, precisely, was seven hundred and fifty dollars. It had cost his father fifteen hundred. When he built it, obtaining half this sum on mortgage, he hoped to pay it up by degrees; but it turned out that, from sickness and other causes, this proved impossible. When, five months before, he had died suddenly, the house, which was all he left, was subject to this incumbrance. Upon this, interest was payable semi-annually at the rate of six per cent. Forty-five dollars a year is not a large sum, but it seemed very large to Mrs. Carter, when added to their necessary expenses for food, clothing and fuel. How it was to be paid she did not exactly see. The same problem had perplexed Herbert, who, like a good son as he was, shared his mother's cares and tried to lighten them. But in a small village like Wrayburn there are not many ways of getting money, at any rate for a boy. There were no manufactories, as in some large villages, and money was a scarce commodity.

Herbert had, however, one source of income. Half a dozen families, living at some distance from the post office, employed him to bring any letters or papers that might come for them, and for this service he received a regular tariff of two cents for each letter, and one cent for each paper. He was not likely to grow rich on this income, but he felt that, though small, it was welcome.

According to custom, Herbert called at the post office on his way home. He found a letter for Deacon Crossleigh, one for Mr. Duncan, two for Dr. Waffit, and papers for each of the two former.

"Ten cents!" he thought with satisfaction. "Well, that is better than nothing, though it won't buy me a new pair of pants."

He was about to leave the office, when the postmaster

called after him: "Wait a minute, Herbert; I believe there's a letter for your mother."

Herbert returned, and received a letter bearing the following superscription: "Mrs. Almira Carter, Wrayburn, New York."

"I hope it isn't bad news," said the postmaster. "I see it's edged with black."

"I can't make out where it's from," said Herbert, scanning the postmark critically.

"Nor I," said the postmaster, rubbing his glasses, and taking another look. "The postmark is very indistinct."

"There's an n and a p," said Herbert, after a little examination. "I think it must be Randolph."

"Randolph? So it is, I declare. Have you got any friends or relatives living there?"

"Yes, my mother's Uncle Herbert, for whom I was named, lives there."

"Then he must be dead."

"What makes you think so?"

"The envelope is edged with black. You had better carry it home before you go round with the others."

"Perhaps I had," said Herbert. "I'll run, so as not to keep the others waiting. Deacon Crossleigh is always in a hurry for his paper."

"Yes, the deacon's always in a fidget to know what's going on, particularly when Congress is in session. He takes a wonderful interest in politics."

Herbert ran up the street with a quick step, pausing a minute at his humble home.

"You are out of breath, Herbert. Have you been running?"

"Yes, I've got a letter for you, and I wanted to bring it before I went round with the rest."

"A letter! Where from?" asked the widow, with curiosity, for she held very little intercourse with the world outside of Wrayburn.

"It's postmarked Randolph, as well as I can make out. While you are reading it, I'll run and leave my letters, and be back to hear the news."

In a hurry to do all his errands and get back, Herbert ran all the way. While his eyes were fixed on one of the envelopes, he ran full against James Leech, who was walking up the street with a pompous air.

In the encounter James's hat came off, and he was nearly thrown down.

"What made you run into me?" he demanded, wrathfully.

"Excuse me, James," said Herbert, recovering himself.

"You did it on purpose," said his enemy, glaring at him angrily.

"That isn't very likely," said Herbert. "I got hit as hard as you did."

"Your hat didn't get knocked off. Pick it up," said James, imperiously, pointing to it as it lay in the path.

"I will, because it is by my fault that it fell," said Herbert, stooping over and picking it up. "You needn't have ordered me to do it."

"The next time take care how you run against a gentleman," said James, arrogantly.

"Take care the next time to speak like a gentleman," said Herbert. "Good night! I must be off."

"Insolent beggar!" muttered James. "He don't know his place. How dare he speak to me in that way?"

CHAPTER II

WHAT THE LETTER CONTAINED

HALF an hour later, Herbert reëntered the cottage, breathless with running.

"Well, mother, what is it?" he asked.

"Uncle Herbert is dead," she answered.

"When did he die?"

"Yesterday morning. They wrote at once. The funeral is to take place to-morrow afternoon, at three o'clock."

"Uncle Herbert was rich, wasn't he, mother?"

"Yes, he must have left nearly a hundred thousand dollars."

"What a pile of money!" said Herbert. "I wonder how a man feels when he is so rich. He ought to be happy."

"Riches don't always bring happiness. Uncle Herbert was disappointed in early life, and that seemed to spoil his career. He gave himself up to money-making, and succeeded in it; but he lived by himself and had few sources of happiness."

"Then he had no family?"

"No."

"Do you think he has left us anything, mother?" asked Herbert, with something of hope in his tone.

"I am afraid not. If he had been disposed to do that he would have done something for us before. He knew that we were poor, and that a little assistance would have been very acceptable. But he never offered it. Even when your father was sick for three months, and I wrote to him for a small loan, he refused, saying that we ought to have laid up money to fall back upon at such a time."

"I don't see how a man can be so unfeeling. If he would only leave us a thousand dollars, how much good it would do us! We could pay up the mortgage on the house, and have something left over. It wouldn't have been much for him to do."

"Well, we won't think too much about it," said Mrs. Carter. "It will be wisest, as probably we should be only preparing ourselves for disappointment. Uncle had a right to do what he pleased with his own."

What the Letter Contained

"Shall you go to the funeral, mother?"

"I don't see how I can," said Mrs. Carter, slowly. "It is twenty miles off, and I am very busy just now. Still one of us ought to go, if only to show respect to so near a relation. People would talk if we didn't. I think, as you were named for your Uncle Herbert, I will let you go."

"If you think best, mother. I will walk, and that will save expense."

"It will be too much for you to take such a walk. You had better ride."

"No, mother, I am young and strong. I can walk well enough."

"But it must be twenty miles," objected his mother.

"The funeral doesn't take place till three o'clock in the afternoon. I will get up bright and early, say at five o'clock. By nine I shall be halfway there."

"I am afraid it will be too much for you, Herbert," said Mrs. Carter, irresolutely.

"You don't know how strong I am," said Herbert; "I shan't get tired so easily as you think."

"But twenty miles is a long distance."

"I know that, but I shall take it easy. The stage fare is seventy-five cents, and it's a good way to save it. I wish somebody would offer me seventy-five cents for every twenty miles I would walk. I'd take it up as a profession."

"I am afraid I could earn little that way. I never was a good walker."

"You're a woman," said Herbert, patronizingly. "Women are not expected to be good walkers."

"Some are. I remember my Aunt Jane would take walks of five and six miles, and think nothing of it."

"I guess I could match her in walking," said Herbert, confidently. "Is she alive?"

"No, she died three years since."

"Perhaps I take after her, then."

"You don't take after me, I am sure of that. I think,

Herbert, you had better take seventy-five cents with you, so that if you get very tired with your walk over, you can come back by stage."

"All right, mother; I'll take the money, but I shall be sure not to need it."

"It is best to be prepared for emergencies, Herbert."

"If I am going to-morrow morning, I must split up enough wood to last you while I am gone."

"I am afraid you will tire yourself. I think I can get along with what wood there is already split."

"Oh, don't be afraid for me. You'll see I'll come back as fresh as when I set out. I expect to have a stunning appetite, though."

"I'll try to cook up enough for you," said his mother, smiling.

Herbert went out into the wood shed, and went to work with great energy at the wood pile. In the course of an hour he had sawed and split several large baskets full, which he brought in and piled up behind the kitchen stove.

Mrs. Carter could not be expected to feel very deep grief for the death of her uncle. It was now more than six years since they had met. He was a selfish man, wholly wrapped up in the pursuit of wealth. Had he possessed benevolent instincts, he would have offered to do something out of his abundance for his niece, who he knew found it very hard to make both ends meet. But he was a man who was very much averse to parting with his money while he lived. He lived on a tenth of his income, and saved up the rest, though for what end he could not well have told. Since the death of Mr. Carter, whose funeral he had not taken the trouble to attend, though invited, he had not even written to his niece, and she had abstained from making any advances, lest it might be thought that she was seeking assistance. Under these circumstances she had little hope of a legacy, though she could not help admitting the thought of how much a few hundred dollars would help her, bridging over the time till Herbert should be old enough to earn fair wages in some employment. If he could study two or three years longer, she would have been very glad, for her son had already shown abilities of no common order; but that was hardly to be thought of.

"There, mother, I guess I've sawed wood enough to last you, unless you are very extravagant," said Herbert, reëntering the kitchen, and taking off his cap. "Now is there anything else I can do? You know I shall be gone two days, or a day and a half at any rate."

"I think of nothing, Herbert. You had better go to bed early, and get a good night's rest, for you will have a hard day before you."

"So I will, but eight o'clock will be soon enough. Just suppose we should get a legacy, after all, mother. Wouldn't it be jolly?"

"I wouldn't think too much of it, Herbert. There isn't much chance of it. Besides, it doesn't seem right to be speculating about our own personal advantage when Uncle Herbert lies dead in his house."

There was justice in this suggestion, but Herbert could hardly be expected to take a mournful view of the death of a relative whom he hardly remembered, and who had appeared scarcely to be aware of his existence. It was natural that the thought of his wealth should be uppermost in his young nephew's mind. The reader will hardly be surprised to hear that Herbert, knowing only too well the disadvantages of poverty, should have speculated a little about his uncle's property after he went to bed. Indeed, it did not leave him even with his waking consciousness. He dreamed that his uncle left him a big lump of gold, so big and heavy that he could not lift it. He was considering anxiously how in the world he was going to get it home, when all at once he awoke, and heard the church clock strike five.

"Time I was on my way!" he thought, and, jumping

out of bed, he dressed himself as quickly as possible, and went downstairs. But, early as it was, his mother was down before him. There was a fire in the kitchen stove, and the cloth was laid for breakfast.

"What made you get up so early, mother?" asked Herbert.

"I wouldn't have you go away without breakfast, Herbert, especially for such a long walk."

"I meant to take something from the closet. That would have done well enough."

"You will be all the better for a good, warm cup of tea. Sit right down. It is all ready."

Early as it was, the breakfast tasted good. Herbert ate hastily, for he was anxious to be on his way. Knowing that he could not afford to buy lunch, he put the remnants of the breakfast, including some slices of bread and butter and meat, into his satchel, and started on his long walk.

CHAPTER III

HERBERT MEETS A RELATIVE

HERBERT had never been to Randolph. In fact, he had never been so far away from Wrayburn. He was not afraid of losing his way, however. Here and there along the road guideposts were conveniently placed, and these removed any difficulty on that score.

When he had gone about six miles, the coach rattled by. It had started more than an hour later. Herbert turned out for the lumbering vehicle, and waited for it to pass. There was a boy on top, but such was the cloud of dust that he could not at first recognize him. It happened, however, that one of the traces broke, so that the driver was compelled to make a stop just as he overtook our hero. Then he saw that the boy on top was James Leech.

Herbert Meets a Relative

With James curiosity overcame his disinclination to speak to one so far beneath him.

"Where are you going, Carter?" he inquired.

"To Randolph," was the answer.

"Going to walk all the way?"

"I expect to," said Herbert, not relishing the cross-examination.

"Why don't you ride?"

James did not ask for information. He knew well enough already, but as there are purse-proud men, so there are boys who are actuated by feelings equally unworthy, and it delighted him to remind Herbert of his poverty. Herbert divined this, but he was proud in his way, and answered: "Because I choose."

"Well, you must like the dust, that's all," said James, complacently tapping his well-polished boot with a light cane which he had bought.

"Where are you going?" asked Herbert, thinking it about time for him to commence questioning.

"I'm going to Randolph, too," answered James, with unwonted affability. "I'm going to stop a few days with a friend of mine, Tom Spencer. His father's a rich man—got a nice place there. Didn't you ever hear of Mr. Spencer, the lawyer?"

"I don't think I have."

"That's his father. He makes a load of money by his law business. I think I shall study law some time. Perhaps I'll go into partnership with him. What are you going to be?"

"I don't know yet," said Herbert.

"I suppose you'll be a mechanic of some kind—a carpenter, or mason, or bricklayer."

"Perhaps so," said Herbert, quietly.

"What are you going to Randolph for?" asked James, with sudden curiosity.

"To attend my uncle's funeral."

"What's your uncle's name?"

"The same as mine."

"I suppose he was poor."

"No, he was rich."

"Was he?" repeated James, in some surprise. "What do you think he was worth?"

"About a hundred thousand dollars."

"Sho! you don't say so. Perhaps," continued James, with new-born respect, "he has left you something in his will."

"I don't think so."

"Why not?"

"He hasn't shown any interest in us for six years, and I don't think he'll remember us now."

James looked thoughtful. He had never before heard of this relationship, or he would have treated Herbert differently. The mere fact of having a wealthy relative elevated our hero considerably in his eyes. Then, too, there was a possibility that Herbert would turn out a legatee.

"When is your uncle's funeral?" he inquired, after a pause.

"This afternoon."

"You won't get there in time. You had better get up and ride."

"No, I guess not."

"Well, perhaps I shall meet you at Randolph."

By this time the harness was repaired, the driver resumed his seat, and whipped up the horses to make up for lost time.

"I'm glad I don't think as much of money as James Leech," thought Herbert. "I suppose if my uncle would only leave us a good round sum, he would forget that I once wore patched pants, and accept me as his intimate friend."

This was exactly what James would have done, and

Herbert Meets a Relative

Herbert showed that he was not wholly without knowledge of the world in forming the conjecture.

Pausing occasionally to rest, Herbert at length accomplished his journey, arriving at Randolph a little after noon. He stopped just outside the village and ate his frugal dinner, which by this time he was prepared to relish. He then took off his jacket and beat the dust out of it, dusted his shoes, and washed his face in a little brook by the roadside. Having thus effaced the marks of travel, he entered the village and inquired the way to the residence of his late uncle. He found out where it was, but did not go there yet, knowing that there would be preparations going on for the funeral. Neither did he go to the tavern, for he knew that he would be expected to dine there, and this was an expense which he did not feel able to incur. He threw himself down in the shade of a tree, and remained there until after he heard the church clock strike two. He was still lying there when a young man, smartly dressed, sporting a showy watch chain and locket and an immense necktie, came up the street and accosted him.

"I say, boy, can you tell me where old man Carter's house is?"

"Yes," said Herbert. "Do you want to go there?"

"Of course I do. I'm one of the relatives. I've come all the way from New York to attend the funeral."

"I'm one of the relations, too," said Herbert. "We'll go along together."

"By Jove, that's strange! How are you related to the old chap?" drawled the young man.

"He was my mother's uncle."

"Was he? Well, I'm a second or third cousin, I don't know which. Never saw him to my knowledge. In fact, I wouldn't have come on to the funeral if I hadn't heard that he was rich. Expect to be remembered?"

"I don't think so. He hasn't taken any notice of mother or myself for years."

"Indeed!" said the young man, who was rather pleased to hear this intelligence. "Are there many relations, do you know?"

"I don't think there are."

"That's good. It makes our chance better, you know. I say, what's your name?"

"Herbert Carter."

"Same as the old man's?"

"Yes."

"Did he know you was named for him?"

"Of course."

"Then he may leave you something for the name," suggested the other, not very well pleased.

"I don't expect anything. What is your name?"

"Cornelius Dixon. I'm related to the old man on my mother's side."

"Are you in business in New York?" asked Herbert, who, in spite of the queer manners of his new relative, felt considerable respect for one who hailed from so important a city.

"Yes, I'm a salesman in a New York store. Where do you live?"

"In Wrayburn."

"Where's that?"

"About twenty miles from here."

"Some one-horse country town, I suppose. Are you in any business?"

"No," said Herbert, "but I'd like to be. Do you think you could get me a place in New York?"

"Well," said Cornelius, flattered by the belief in his influence which this inquiry implied, "perhaps I might. You can give me your name and address, so I can write to you if I hear of anything. If the old man only leaves me a few thousand dollars, I'll go into business for myself, and then I'd have an opening for you."

"I hope he will, then."

of the deceased. For years she had lived on a small pension from her brother, increased somewhat by knitting stockings for the neighbors. She, indeed, was the only real mourner. The rest were speculating about how far they were likely to be benefited by the death of the deceased, of whom they had seen but little in life. Even Herbert, though impressed by the presence of death, could hardly be expected to feel deep grief for a man who had neglected his mother in his life.

Of the funeral rites it is unnecessary to speak. We are interested in what came afterwards.

The relations were quietly notified to meet at five o'clock in the office of Mr. Spencer, the lawyer, to whom had been intrusted the will of the late Mr. Carter. Those who have even a slight knowledge of human nature will not need to be told that the attendance of all was punctual. There was an anxious, expectant look on the faces of all—not even excepting the old lady. She knew that if her brother had made no provision for her, she must go to the almshouse, and against this her honest pride revolted. She was willing to live on anything, however little, if she might live independently, as she had hitherto done. To feel herself dependent on public charity would indeed have been a hard trial for the poor old lady. Of all, probably Mrs. Pinkerton was the most confident. She had come to feel that her family was entitled to a large share of the estate, and she had gone so far as to decide just how she would invest it, and what new arrangements she would make, for she had no idea of consulting her husband on the subject.

The lawyer was a gentlemanly-looking man, whose face inspired confidence in his integrity—a remark which, unhappily, cannot be made of all in his profession. He took his seat at a table, and produced the will, which he considerately commenced reading at once. After the usual introduction, the will proceeded thus:

"To my sister Nancy I give the use of my house, rent free, as long as she shall live. I leave her also an income of two hundred dollars a year, which, as her wants are small, will be sufficient to maintain her in comfort."

The old lady breathed a sigh of relief. Her fears were removed. She could continue to live as she had been accustomed to do, and need not be beholden to private or public charity. Mrs. Pinkerton was not so well pleased. She felt almost as if she had been deprived of what belonged to her by right. She frowned at Miss Nancy, but the old lady was unconscious of the displeasure excited in the bosom of her imposing-looking relative.

The lawyer proceeded: "To my cousin, Alonzo Granger, I leave one hundred dollars; not because he needs it, for I understand that he is well-to-do, but as a mark of remembrance."

The farmer scowled slightly, and opened and closed his brown hands in dissatisfaction. He was well-to-do; but when was a man ever satisfied with that? He had counted upon a few thousands, with which he proposed to buy an adjoining farm. Mrs. Pinkerton, however, was pleased. There was so much the more for her.

"To Cornelius Dixon"—here Herbert's morning acquaintance began to feel excited—"I bequeath one hundred dollars, to buy a looking-glass and a new suit of clothes."

The young man's face lengthened very perceptibly as he heard the small amount of his legacy, and he glared savagely at Mrs. Pinkerton, who showed a mirthful face at his discomfiture.

Her turn came next.

Reading the Will

"To Josiah Pinkerton, his wife and children, I leave one hundred dollars apiece; also my best black pantaloons, which he or his wife may appropriate, as may be arranged between them."

All except the Pinkertons laughed at this sly hit, and even the lawyer smiled; but the stout lady flushed with rage and disappointment, and ejaculated: "Abominable!" The eyes of all were now directed to Herbert, who was the only one remaining. Could it be possible that the balance of the property was left to him? The fear of this made him the focus of unfriendly eyes, and he became restive and anxious.

"To my namesake, Herbert Carter, I leave a black trunk which I keep in my room, with all that it contains. To his mother I direct that the sum of one hundred dollars be paid."

This was not much, but it was more than Herbert had expected. He knew how welcome even one hundred dollars would be to his mother, and he looked satisfied—the only one of the party, except the old lady, who showed any pleasure at the contents of the will.

The relatives looked bewildered. All had been mentioned in turn, and yet but a small part—a very small part—of the estate had been disposed of. Mrs. Pinkerton bluntly expressed the general curiosity.

"Who's to have the rest, Mr. Spencer?" she demanded.

"I'm coming to that," answered the lawyer, quietly.

"All the rest and residue of my property, of whatever kind, I leave to the town of Randolph, to establish a high school, directing that not more than twenty thousand dollars be expended upon the building, which shall be of brick. I desire that the school shall be known as the Carter

School, to the end that my name may be remembered in connection with what I hope will prove a public blessing."

"That is all," said the lawyer, and he laid down the will upon the table.

CHAPTER V

WHAT CAME AFTERWARD

THERE was silence for a minute after the will was read. Mrs. Pinkerton fanned herself furiously, and looked angry and excited.

At length she said: "I wish to say that that is a very unjust will, Mr. Spencer."

"I am not responsible for it, Mrs. Pinkerton," answered the lawyer, quietly.

"I don't know what the rest of you think," said the angry lady, with a general glance around the office, "but I think the will ought to be broken."

"On what grounds?" asked Mr. Spencer.

"He had no right to put off his own flesh and blood with a beggarly pittance, and leave all his money to the town."

"Pardon me; whatever you may think of Mr. Carter's will, there is no doubt that he had a perfect legal right to dispose of it as he did."

"Then the laws ought to be altered," said Mrs. Pinkerton, angrily. "I don't believe he was sane when he made the will."

"If you can prove that," said the lawyer, "you can set aside the will; but not otherwise."

"My brother was in his right mind," here interposed Miss Nancy. "He always meant to give the town money for a school."

"No doubt you think he was sane," sneered Mrs. Pinkerton, turning upon the old lady. " You have fared better than any of us."

" Miss Nancy was most nearly related to the deceased," said the lawyer, " and she needed help most."

" It's all very well to talk," said the lady, tossing her head, " but me and mine have been badly used. I have hard work enough to support the family, and little help I get from him," she added, pointing to her unhappy husband.

" I'm workin' all the time," remonstrated Josiah. " You are unkind, Maria."

" I could hire a boy to do all your work for three dollars a week," she retorted. " That's all you help me. I've worried along for years, expectin' Mr. Carter would do something handsome for us; and now he's put us off with four hundred dollars."

" I get only one hundred," said the farmer.

" And I, too. It's a beastly shame," remarked Cornelius.

" Really," said the lawyer, " it appears to me unseemly to speak so bitterly so soon after the funeral."

" I dare say you like it well enough," said Mrs. Pinkerton, sharply. " You've got all our money to build a schoolhouse."

" It will not benefit me any more than the townspeople generally," said the lawyer. " For my part, I should have been glad if my late friend had left a larger sum to those connected with him by blood."

" Don't you think we could break the will? " asked Mrs. Pinkerton, persuasively. " Couldn't you help us? "

" You can attempt it, but I assure you in advance you haven't the ghost of a chance. You would only lose your money, for the town would strenuously oppose you."

The stout lady's face fell. She felt that the last hope was gone.

" All I can say is, that it's a scandalous thing," she concluded, bitterly.

"I should like to know what's in that trunk he left you," said Cornelius Dixon, turning to Herbert. "Maybe it's money or bonds. If it is, don't forget our agreement."

This drew attention to Herbert.

"To be sure," said Mrs. Pinkerton, whose curiosity was aroused, "Mr. Dixon may be right. Suppose we all go over to the house and open it."

Herbert looked irresolutely toward the lawyer.

"There is no objection, I suppose," said Mr. Spencer.

"I know what's in the trunk," said Miss Nancy.

Straightway all eyes were turned upon her.

"What is it?"

"It's clothes. My brother used to keep his clothes in that trunk."

Cornelius Dixon burst into a rude laugh.

"I say, Herbert, I congratulate you," he said, with a chuckle. "The old fellow's left you his wardrobe. You'll look like a peacock when you put 'em on. If you ever come to New York to see me, leave 'em at home. I wouldn't like to walk up Broadway with such a gawk as you'd look."

"Young man," said Miss Nancy, her voice tremulous, "it don't look well in you to ridicule my poor departed brother. He didn't forget you."

"He might as well," muttered Cornelius.

"I hope you won't laugh at my brother's gift," said the old lady, turning to Herbert.

"No, ma'am," said Herbert, respectfully. "I am glad to get it. I can't afford to buy new clothes often, and they can be made over for me."

"You wouldn't catch me wearing such old-fashioned duds," said Cornelius, scornfully.

"No one asked you to, young man," said the old lady, disturbed at the manner in which her brother was spoken of. "The boy's worth a dozen of you."

"Thank you," said Cornelius, bowing with mock respect. "I should like to ask," he continued, turning to the lawyer, "when I can get my legacy. It isn't much, but I might as well take it."

"As the amount is small, I will send you a check next week," said Mr. Spencer, "if you will leave me your address."

"And can I have my money, too?" demanded Mrs. Pinkerton. "It's a miserable pittance, but I owe it to my poor children to take it."

"I will send your husband a check also, next week, madam."

"You needn't send it to him. You may send it to me," said the lady.

"Part of it is mine," expostulated the husband, in meek deprecation.

"I can give you your part," said his wife. "Mr. Spencer, you may make the check payable to me."

"But, Maria——"

"Be silent, Josiah! Don't make a fool of yourself," said his wife, in an imperious tone.

The poor man was fain to be silent, but the lawyer was indignant, and said: "Mr. Pinkerton, I will certainly not pay your legacy, nor your children's, to anyone but yourself. I will send Mrs. Pinkerton a check for her own share —one hundred dollars—since she desires it."

"I insist upon your sending me the children's money also," said the lady angrily. "He ain't fit to take charge of it."

"You may insist as much as you like, Mrs. Pinkerton," said the lawyer, coolly, "but it will be useless. As the head of the family, I shall send the money designed for the children to your husband."

"Do you call him the head of the family?" demanded the angry Maria. "I would have you to know, sir, that I am the head of the family."

"The law does not recognize you as such. As to the

pantaloons, which form a part of the legacy, I will forward them to you, if you wish."

"Do you mean to insult me, sir?" gasped Mrs. Pinkerton, growing very red in the face.

"Not at all; but they were left either to you or your husband, as you might jointly agree."

The lady was about to decline accepting them at all, but it occurred to her that they might be made over to suit her husband, and so save the expense of a new pair, and she directed that they should be sent to him.

Then, gathering her family about her, she strode majestically from the office, shaking off, metaphorically, the dust of her feet against it.

Next Mr. Granger, after a few words with the lawyer, departed. Mr. Cornelius Dixon also announced that he must depart.

"Come and see me some time in the city," he said to Herbert, "and if you ever get a windfall just put it into my hands, and I'll go into business with you."

"I'll remember," said Herbert, "but I'm afraid it'll be a good while before that."

"I don't know about that. You can open a second-hand clothing store. The old man's left you a good stock in trade. Good joke, isn't it? Good-by."

Next Miss Nancy rose to go.

"Tell your mother to call and see me, my boy," she said, kindly, to Herbert. "I wish my brother'd left her more, for I know she needs it."

"Thank you, Miss Nancy," said Herbert, respectfully; "but we don't complain. We are thankful for what we have received."

"You're the best of 'em," said the old lady, earnestly. "You're a good boy, and God will prosper you."

She went out, and of the eight heirs Herbert alone remained.

CHAPTER VI

THE LAWYER'S HOME

The lawyer regarded Herbert with a smile.

"Your uncle's will doesn't seem to have given general satisfaction," he said.

"No," responded Herbert; "but for my part I have come out as well as I expected."

"I suppose you know Mr. Carter was rich?"

"So my mother told me."

"How much do you think he was worth?"

Herbert was rather surprised at this question. Why should the lawyer ask it, when of course he knew much more about the matter?

"About a hundred thousand dollars, I suppose," he answered.

"You are not far wrong. Now doesn't your share, and your mother's, seem very small compared with this large amount?"

"It is very small compared with that, but we had no claim to anything. The clothes and the money will be very useful to us."

"You are a model heir," said Mr. Spencer, smiling. "You alone do not find fault, except, of course, Miss Nancy, who has fared the best."

"I would rather make a fortune for myself than inherit one from another," said Herbert, sturdily.

"I respect your independence, my boy," said the lawyer, who felt favorably disposed toward our hero. "Still, a legacy isn't to be despised. Now tell me when you want to take your trunk."

"I want to ask your advice about that," said Herbert. "I walked over from Wrayburn. How shall I carry the trunk back?"

"You will have to return by the stage to-morrow morning, that is, if you are ready to go back so soon."

"Do they charge much to stop overnight at the hotel?" asked Herbert, anxiously, for he had but seventy-five cents with him. It occurred to him how foolish he had been not to consider that it would be necessary for him to spend the night in Randolph.

"I don't know exactly how much. I think they charge fifty cents for a bed, and the same for each meal."

Herbert's face lengthened, and he became alarmed. How was he going to manage, on his limited resources?

The lawyer penetrated his perplexity, and, being a kind-hearted man, quickly came to his relief.

"I think you would find it lonely at the hotel, my boy," he said, "and I shall therefore invite you to pass the night at my house instead."

"You are very kind, sir," said Herbert, gratefully, finding his difficulty happily removed. "I accept your invitation with pleasure."

"The boy has been well brought up, if he is poor," thought Mr. Spencer. "Well," he said, "that is settled. I think our supper must be ready, so we will go over to the house at once. By the way, there is a boy from your town visiting my son. You must know him?"

"Is it James Leech?" asked Herbert, remembering what James had told him.

"Yes. Do you know him?"

"We are schoolmates."

"Then it will be pleasant for you to meet."

Herbert was not quite sure about this, but forbore to say so.

He accompanied Mr. Spencer to his house, which was just across the street from the office, and followed the lawyer into an apartment handsomely furnished. James Leech and Tom Spencer were sitting at a small table, playing checkers.

"Hello, Carter!" exclaimed James, in surprise, "how came you here?"

"Mr. Spencer invited me," said Herbert, not surprised at the mode of address.

"Did your uncle leave you anything?" asked James, with interest.

"Yes."

"How much?"

"He left my mother a hundred dollars."

"That isn't much," said James, contemptuously. "Was that all?"

"No, he left me a trunk, and what is in it."

"What is in it?"

"Clothes, I believe."

"A lot of old clothes!" commented James, turning up his nose. "That's a fine legacy, I must say."

"I shall find them useful," said Herbert, quietly.

"Oh, no doubt. You can roll up the pants and coat-sleeves. It will be fun to see you parading round in your uncle's tailcoats."

"I don't think you'll have that pleasure," said Herbert, flushing. "If I wear them I shall have them made over for me."

"I congratulate you on your new and extensive wardrobe," said James, mockingly. "Won't you cut a dash, though, on the streets of Wrayburn!"

Herbert did not deign a reply to this rude speech. Tom Spencer, who was much more of a gentleman than James, was disgusted with his impertinence. He rose, and took Herbert by the hand.

"You must let me introduce myself," he said. "My name is Thomas Spencer, and I am glad to see you here."

"Thank you," said Herbert, his heart opening at the frank and cordial manner of the other. "My name is Herbert Carter, and I am very glad to make your acquaintance."

"Are you going to finish this game, Tom?" drawled James, not relishing the idea of Herbert's receiving any attention from his friend.

"If you don't mind, we'll have it another time," said Tom. "There goes the supper bell, and I for one am hungry."

At the supper table James noticed, to his secret disgust, that Herbert was treated with as much consideration as himself. Mr. and Mrs. Spencer appeared to consider them social equals, which made James very uncomfortable.

"You boys are about of an age, I suppose," said Mr. Spencer.

"I really don't know," said James, haughtily.

"You attend the same school?"

"Yes," said James, "but I expect to go to some select academy very soon. At a public school you have to associate with all classes, you know."

Mr. Spencer arched his brows, and steadily regarded the young aristocrat.

"I don't see any great distinction of classes in a country village," said he, dryly. "Besides, we are living in a republic."

"You wouldn't like to associate on equal terms with a day laborer," said James, pertly.

"I am a laborer myself," said the lawyer, smiling. "I wish I could say I were a day laborer exclusively, but sometimes I have to work into the night."

"You are a professional man, and a gentleman," said James. "You don't work with your hands."

"I hope you boys will all grow up gentlemen," said Mr. Spencer.

"I shall, of course," said James.

"And you, Tom?"

"I hope so."

"And you, Herbert?"

"I hope so, too," said Herbert; "but if it is necessary to be rich to be a gentleman, I am not sure about it."

"What is your idea of a gentleman, James?" asked the lawyer.

"He must be of a good family, and wear good clothes, and live nicely."

"Is that all?"

"He ought to be well educated."

"I see you name that last which I should name first. So these constitute a gentleman, in your opinion?"

"Yes, sir."

"Not always. I have known men combining all the qualifications you have mentioned, who were very far from being gentlemen, in my opinion."

"How is that, sir?" asked James, puzzled.

"They were arrogant, puffed up with an idea of their own importance, deficient in politeness."

"How well he has described James!" thought Herbert, but he was too much of a gentleman to say so.

James looked disconcerted, and dropped the subject. He thought the lawyer had some queer ideas. Why need a gentleman be polite to his inferiors? he thought, but he didn't say so.

After supper the boys went out behind the house, and feasted on peaches, which were just ripe. Herbert found Tom very social, but James took very little notice of him. Our hero did not make himself unhappy on this account. In fact, he was in unusual good spirits, and enjoyed in anticipation the pleasure of going back to Wrayburn with the welcome news of the two legacies.

About half past seven Mr. Spencer came out into the orchard.

"As the stage starts early in the morning, Herbert," he said, "we had better go over and get the trunk ready, so that you can take it home."

James Leech hoped to receive an invitation to accompany the two; but no invitation was given, and he was forced to content himself with staying behind.

CHAPTER VII

A WELCOME DISCOVERY

Mr. Spencer entered the house so lately vacated by the old man who had occupied it for forty years.

"The trunk is in your uncle's room," said the lawyer, "or ought to be. I suppose it has not been moved."

The two entered the chamber. It was a small, poorly furnished apartment, covered with a carpet which, cheap in the first place, was so worn with use that the bare floor showed in spots.

"Your uncle was not very luxurious in his taste," said Mr. Spencer. "There are plenty of day laborers in town who have as good rooms as this."

"I suppose he liked laying up money better than spending it," said Herbert.

"You are right there. This must be the trunk."

It was a small, black hair trunk, studded with brass nails. Mr. Spencer took a bunch of keys from his pocket and unlocked it. Lifting the cover he exposed to view a collection of woolen clothes—coats, vests, and pants.

"This is your legacy, Herbert," said the lawyer. "I am afraid you won't find it very valuable. What is this?"

He drew out, and held up to view, a blue cloak of ample proportions.

"Will you try it on?" he said, smiling.

Herbert threw it over his shoulders, and looked at himself in a small seven-by-nine looking-glass which was suspended over the washstand. It came down nearly to his feet.

A Welcome Discovery

"I should hardly dare to wear this without alteration," he said; "but there is a good deal of good cloth in it. Mother can cut a coat and vest out of it for me."

"Here is a blue coat with brass buttons. I remember your uncle used to wear it to church twenty years ago. Of late years he has not attended, and has had no occasion to wear it. Here is a pair of pantaloons; but they are pretty well worn."

So they went through the list, finding little of value. The last article was a vest.

"It seems heavy," said Herbert.

The lawyer took it from him and examined it.

"There seems to be an inside pocket," he said. "There must be something in it."

The pocket was confined by a button; Mr. Spencer thrust his fingers inside, and drew out something loosely enveloped in brown paper.

"What have we here?" he said, in a tone of curiosity.

The secret was speedily solved. When the paper was opened, it was found to contain five gold eagles, and two dollars in silver coins.

Herbert's eyes glistened with delight as he viewed the treasure.

"Fifty-two dollars!" he exclaimed. "And it is mine."

"Undoubtedly. The will expressly says you are to have the trunk, and all it contains."

"I wonder whether Uncle Herbert remembered this money?"

"We can't tell as to that, but it doesn't affect your title to the money. I congratulate you, Herbert."

"It will do us a great deal of good. Then there are the hundred dollars for mother. Why, we shall be rich."

"Then you are content with your legacy?" asked Mr. Spencer.

"Oh, yes; it was more than I expected, or mother, either."

"Yet it is but a mere drop of your uncle's wealth," said the lawyer, thoughtfully.

"That may be; but he needn't have left us anything."

"I see you look upon it in the best way. You are quite a model heir—very different from most of your relatives—Mrs. Pinkerton, for instance."

"I supposed she expected more than I did."

"She appeared to expect the bulk of the property. I am afraid her husband will have a hard time of it for a week to come," said the lawyer, laughing. He will have to bear the brunt of her disappointment. Well, there seems no more for us to do here. We have found out the value of your legacy, and may lock the trunk again. If you will lend a hand, we will take it across to my house, so that there may be no delay when the stage calls in the morning."

"All right, sir."

James Leech was looking out of the front window, awaiting the return of Mr. Spencer and Herbert with not a little curiosity. At length he spied them.

"Tom!" he exclaimed, "your father and that Carter boy are coming back."

"Why do you call him that Carter boy? Why don't you call him Herbert?"

"I am not on intimate terms with him," said James.

"That is strange, as you both live in the same village."

"You must remember that there is some difference in our social positions," said James, haughtily.

"That is something I never think of," said Tom, candidly. "I am a genuine republican."

"I am not," said James. "I should like to live in England, where they have noblemen."

"Not unless you could be a nobleman yourself, I suppose?"

"No; of course not."

A Welcome Discovery

By this time Mr. Spencer and Herbert were bringing the trunk into the front entry.

"I shouldn't think a professional gentleman like your father would like to be seen carrying a trunk across the street," said James.

"Oh, he don't care for that; nor should I," said Tom.

Herbert entered the room.

"Well, Herbert, what luck?" asked Tom.

"Better than I expected," said Herbert, gayly. "What do you say to that?" and he displayed the gold and silver.

"How much is it?" asked James, his vanity melting under the influence of curiosity.

"Fifty-two dollars."

"Capital!" said Tom.

"It isn't much," said James, in a tone of depreciation.

"I'll bet Herbert is richer than you, James," said Tom, in a lively manner. "Can you show as much money as that?"

"I shall be a rich man some day," said James, with an air of importance.

"Your father may fail."

"The moon may be made of green cheese," retorted James, loftily. "How about the clothes? Are you going to show them?"

"I think not," said Herbert.

"A parcel of rags, I suppose," said James, with a sneer.

"Not quite so bad as that," responded Herbert, good-naturedly. "Still, I think I shall hardly venture to wear any of them without alteration."

"I wouldn't wear second-hand clothes," remarked James Leech, in his usual amiable tone.

"Perhaps you would if you were poor," said Herbert, quietly.

"But I am not poor."

"Fortunately for you."

"Then you won't show the clothes? I suppose they look as if they were made in the year one."

"For our forefather Adam?" suggested Tom, laughing. "I am inclined to think the old gentleman in question hadn't clothes enough to fill a trunk as large as that."

"Probably not," said Herbert; "he had no uncle, you know, to leave any to him."

"What are you going to do with your money, Carter?" asked James, whose curiosity got the better of his dignity occasionally.

"I haven't made up my mind yet. I think I shall find plenty of uses for it."

"What would you do with it if you had it, James?" asked Tom.

"I can have more if I want to. I have only to ask father."

"Then you're better off than I. Say, father, will you give me fifty-two dollars?"

"When you are twenty-one I may do it."

"You see," said Tom. "But you haven't answered my question. What would you do with the money if you had it?"

"I think I would buy a new rowboat; there's a pond near our house."

"When you get it send for me, and I'll help you row."

"Very well," said James; but he did not answer very positively. In fact, he was by no means sure that his father would comply with his request for money, although it suited him to make this representation to his companions.

Herbert retired early. It had been a fatiguing day for him, and it would be necessary to rise in good season the next day, as the coach left Randolph for Wrayburn at an early hour.

CHAPTER VIII

HERBERT'S RETURN

Mrs. Carter awaited Herbert's return with interest. She felt lonely without him, for he had never before been away from home to stay overnight. But there was a feeling of anticipation besides. Her hopes of a legacy were not very strong, but of course there was a possibility of her uncle's having remembered them in his will.

"Even if it is only five dollars, it will be welcome," she thought. "Where people are so poor as we are, every little helps."

She sat at her sewing when the stage stopped before the door.

"I'm glad he rode home," thought the widow; "the walk both ways would have been too fatiguing."

"But why does not Herbert come in at once?"

He had gone behind the coach, and the driver was helping him take down a trunk."

"Where did he get it?" thought his mother, in surprise.

"I guess you can get it into the house yourself," she heard the driver say.

"Yes, I'll manage it; you needn't wait," said Herbert.

The driver cracked his whip, and the lumbering old coach drove on.

"Oh, there you are, mother," said Herbert, looking toward the house for the first time. "I'll be with you in a minute."

And he began to draw the trunk in through the front gate.

"Where did you get that trunk, Herbert?" asked Mrs. Carter.

"Oh, it's my legacy," said Herbert, laughing. "Here

it is," and he lifted it up, and laid it down in the front entry.

"What is inside?" asked his mother, with natural curiosity.

"It isn't full of gold and silver, mother, so don't raise your expectations too high. It contains some clothes of Uncle Herbert, out of which you can get some for me."

"I am glad of that, for you need some new clothes. Well, we were not forgotten, after all."

"You don't seem disappointed, mother."

"I might have wished for a little money besides, Herbert; but beggars cannot be choosers."

"But sometimes they get what they wish for. Uncle Herbert left you a legacy of a hundred dollars."

"A hundred dollars!" said Mrs. Carter, brightly. "Why, that will be quite a help for us. Was it left to me?"

"Yes, to you."

"It was kind in your uncle. My legacy is more than yours, Herbert."

"I don't know about that, mother; look here!"

And Herbert displayed his gold and silver.

"Here are fifty-two dollars that I found in the pocket of a vest. It belongs to me, for the will says expressly that I am to have the trunk and all it contains."

"I am really glad," said his mother, joyfully. "We are more fortunate than I expected. Sit down and tell me all about it. Who got the bulk of the property?"

"None of the relations. It is bequeathed to the town of Randolph, to found a high school, to be called the Carter School."

"Well, it will do good, at any rate. Didn't the other relations receive legacies?"

"Small ones; but they didn't seem very well satisfied. Do you know Mr. and Mrs. Josiah Pinkerton?"

Herbert's Return

"Slightly," said Mrs. Carter, smiling. "Were they there?"

"She was, and he was in attendance upon her. She didn't give him a chance to say much."

"I have always heard she kept him in good subjection. How did they fare?"

"They and their two children received a hundred dollars apiece. She was mad and wanted to break the will. Then there was a Mr. Granger, a farmer, who got the same; and Cornelius Dixon, also."

"I hope Aunt Nancy fared better. She is the best of them all."

"She is allowed to occupy the house, rent free, and is to have an income of two hundred dollars a year as long as she lives."

"I am really glad to hear it," said Mrs. Carter, with emphasis. "She deserves all her good fortune. One of the best things her brother did in life was to allow her such an income as to keep her independent of public charity; I feared he would forget to provide for her."

"She seems a good old lady. She asked me to invite you to call and see her."

"I should like to do so, and if I ever have occasion to go to Randolph I will certainly do so."

"Now, mother," said Herbert, when he had answered his mother's questions, "I want you to take this money, and use it as you need."

"But, Herbert, it was left to you."

"And if you use it I shall receive my share of it. By the way, your money will be sent you next week; so Mr. Spencer assured me."

"Who is Mr. Spencer?"

"The lawyer who read the will. He was very kind to me. It was at his house I spent the night. I got acquainted with his son, Tom, a fine fellow. I met also

James Leech, whom I cannot compliment so highly. He was visiting Tom."

"I never thought him an agreeable boy."

"Nor anyone else, I expect. He appears to think he can put on airs, and expects everybody to bow down to him because his father is a rich man."

"I hope you didn't quarrel with him," said Mrs. Carter, apprehensively.

"Oh, no; he sneered at me, as usual, and drew a ridiculous picture of my appearance with my uncle's clothes on."

"Do you mind what he says?" asked his mother, anxiously.

"A little," said Herbert; "but I can stand it if he doesn't go too far."

"He has an unhappy nature. I think his father must have been somewhat like him when he was young."

"So do I. He feels just as important as James. I like to see him strut round, as if he owned the whole village."

"He does own more of it than anyone else. Among the rest, he owns our house, in part."

"You mean he has a mortgage on it, mother?"

"Yes."

"Seven hundred and fifty dollars, isn't it?"

"Yes, Herbert."

"How much do you consider the whole worth?" asked our hero, thoughtfully.

"It cost your father fifteen hundred dollars. That is, the land—nearly an acre—cost three hundred dollars, and the house, to build, twelve hundred."

"Would it sell for that?"

"Not if a sale were forced; but, if anybody wanted it, fifteen hundred dollars would not be too much to pay."

"I wish the mortgage were paid."

"So do I, my son; but we are not very likely to be able to pay it."

"How fine it would have been if Uncle Herbert had left

Herbert's Return

us, say eight hundred dollars, so that we might have paid it up, and still have had a little left for immediate use!"

"Yes, Herbert, it would have made us feel quite independent, but it isn't best speculating on what might have been. It is better to do the best we can with what we really have."

"I suppose you are right, mother; but it is pleasant to dream of good fortune, even if we know it is out of reach."

"The trouble is, our dreaming often interferes with our working."

"It shan't interfere with mine. I've got something to work for."

"Do you refer to anything in particular, Herbert?"

"Yes. I want to pay off this mortgage," answered Herbert, manfully.

"Some day, when you are a man, you may be able; but the time is too far off to spend much time upon it at present."

Herbert had moved to the window as the conversation went on. Suddenly he called to his mother: "Look, mother, there is Squire Leech riding up. He is pointing out our house to the man that is riding with him. Do you know who it is?"

"Yes, it is Mr. Banks, his new superintendent. He has just come into the village."

"I wonder why he pointed at our house?"

"Probably he was telling him that he had a mortgage on it."

"When does the interest come due on the mortgage?"

"Next week. I had only five dollars laid by to meet it, but, thanks to my legacy, I shall have no trouble in the matter."

"If you couldn't pay the interest, could the squire foreclose?"

"Yes, that's the law, I believe."

"And he would take advantage of it. But he never shall, if I can prevent it."

CHAPTER IX

A BUSINESS CONFIDENCE

Squire Leech lived in a large, square, white house, situated on an eminence some way back from the street. It had bay windows on either side of the front door, a gravel walk, bordered with flowers, leading to the gate, a small summerhouse on the lawn, and altogether was much the handsomest residence in the village. Three years before, the house, or, at all events, the principal rooms, had been newly furnished from the city. No wonder the squire and all the family held up their heads, and regarded themselves as belonging to the aristocracy.

In a back room, used partly as a sitting room, partly as an office, the great man and his new superintendent, Amos Banks, were sitting, the evening previous to Herbert's return home. It may be asked why Squire Leech needed a superintendent. To this I answer that his property, beside the home farm, included two outlying farms, which he preferred to carry on himself rather than let to tenants. Besides, he had stocks and bonds, to which he himself attended. But the farms required more attention than he individually was willing to bestow. Accordingly he employed a competent man, who had the general supervision of them. His former superintendent having emigrated to the West, he had engaged Mr. Banks, who had been recommended to him for the charge. Banks came from a town thirty miles distant, and had never lived in Wrayburn before. He had just entered upon his duties, and was talking over business matters with the squire.

"You will occupy the house on the Ross farm," said

Squire Leech. "I think you will find it comfortable. I have always reserved it for my superintendent."

"There is a house on the other farm, I suppose," said Banks.

"Yes; but that is occupied by a family already. I don't rent the farm, that is, except about half an acre of land for a kitchen garden. That I have prepared to cultivate myself."

"Precisely," said the superintendent. "I will tell you why I inquired. You tell me there will be need of another permanent farm workman. Now I know an excellent man —in fact, he is a cousin of my own—who would be glad to accept the place."

"Very well. I have no objection to your engaging him, since you vouch for him."

"Oh, yes; he is a faithful and industrious man, and he will be willing to do work for moderate wages. Indeed, he cares more for a permanent place than high pay. Where he is now, he is liable to be idle for some months in the year."

"Is he a family man?"

"Yes; he has two young children."

"Of course he will move to Wrayburn."

"Yes; if he can get a suitable house. In fact, that was what I was coming at. I thought of your other house, but you say that is already occupied."

"Yes; and the family has occupied it for several years. I should not like to dislodge them."

"Do you know any other small house my cousin could rent?"

Squire Leech reflected.

"The fact is," he said, after a pause, "there has not been much building going on in Wrayburn for several years, and it is hard to find a vacant house."

"I am sorry for that. I am afraid it may interfere with Brown's coming."

"There is one house, I think, that would just suit your cousin," said Squire Leech, slowly.

"Where is it?"

"It is now occupied by the widow Carter and her son."

"Is she going to move?"

"She wouldn't like to."

"Then how will that help us? Who owns the house?"

"She does; that is, nominally. I hold a mortgage on the place for seven hundred and fifty dollars, which is more than half the market value."

"Then it may eventually fall into your hands?"

"Very probably. Between ourselves, I think it probable that she will fail to be ready with the semi-annual interest, which comes due next week. She is quite poor—has nothing but this property—and has to sew for a living, or braid straw, neither of which pays well."

"Suppose she is not ready with the interest, do you propose to foreclose?"

"I think I shall. I will allow her three or four hundred dollars for her share of the property, and that will be the best thing she can do, in my opinion."

Whether or not it would be the best thing for Mrs. Carter, it certainly wouldn't be a bad speculation for the squire, since the place, as already stated, was worth fully fifteen hundred dollars. How a rich man can deliberately plot to defraud a poor woman of a portion of her small property, you and I, my young reader, may find it hard to understand. Unfortunately there are too many cases in real life where just such things happen, so that there really seems to be a good deal of truth in the old adage that prosperity hardens the heart.

If Mr. Banks had been a just or kind-hearted man, he would not have encouraged his employer in the plan he had just broached; but he was selfish, and thought he saw in it an easy solution of the difficulty which he had met with in securing a house for his cousin. He did not know

A Business Confidence

Mrs. Carter, and felt no particular interest in the question what was to become of her if she was ejected from her house. No doubt she would find a home somewhere. At any rate, it was not his business.

"It seems to me that will be an excellent plan," he said, with satisfaction. "How soon can we find out about it?"

"Next week—Tuesday. It is then that the interest comes due."

"Suppose she is ready to pay the interest, what then?"

"Then I will make her an offer for the place, and represent to her that it will be the better plan for her to part with it, and so escape the payment of interest. She has to pay forty-five dollars a year, and that is a great drain upon one who earns no more than she does."

"I think you said she had a son; does he earn anything? Or perhaps he isn't old enough."

"Yes, he is thirteen or fourteen; still, there isn't much in a small village like this for a boy to do. He is attending school, I believe."

"Then, in one way or another, you think there is a good chance of our obtaining the house," said the superintendent, with satisfaction.

"Yes, I think so."

"How would it do to go around and speak to the widow about it beforehand? I could then write to Brown."

"As to that, she may be very particular to retain the house, and even if she is not provided with the money, succeed in borrowing enough. Now, my idea is to say nothing about it till Tuesday. She may depend upon my waiting a few days. That I shall not do. If the money is not forthcoming I will foreclose at once, without giving her time to arrange for the money."

The superintendent nodded.

"A very shrewd plan, Squire Leech," he said. "By the way, where is the house situated?"

"Only a furlong up the road. It is on the opposite side of the way."

"I think I remember it. There is some land connected with it, isn't there?"

"Nearly an acre. The house is small, but neat. In fact, for a small place, I consider it quite desirable. To-morrow we will ride by it, and you can take more particular notice."

They did ride by, as we know, and Squire Leech pointed it out to his superintendent. Herbert noticed this, but he did not know that the two men had formed a scheme for turning his mother and himself out of their comfortable home, and defrauding his mother of a considerable portion of the small property which his father had left. Had he known this, it would have filled him with indignation, and he would have felt that even property is no absolute safeguard against the selfish schemes of the mercenary and the rapacious.

CHAPTER X

SQUIRE LEECH IS BAFFLED

Tuesday arrived, but as yet the check from Mr. Spencer had not been received.

"Never mind, mother," said Herbert, "you will get it before the end of the week."

"But I shall need it to pay the interest to Squire Leech. He will call for it to-day."

"How much it is?"

"Twenty-two dollars and a half."

"You forget the gold I handed you last week."

"I don't like to use it, Herbert; I want you to use it for yourself."

"I am as much interested in paying the interest as you, mother. Don't I occupy the house?"

Squire Leech is Baffled

Seeing that Herbert was in earnest, Mrs. Carter overcame her scruples, and laid aside enough of the money to make up the amount required.

About five minutes of twelve Squire Leech was seen advancing to the front door with slow, pompous steps.

"There he comes, mother!" said Herbert. "I'll open the door."

"Is your mother at home, Herbert?" asked the squire, in a dignified tone.

"Yes, sir. Won't you walk in?"

"Ahem, yes! I think I will. I have a little matter of business with her."

Squire Leech entered the small sitting room, which seemed uncomfortably full when he was in it—not on account of his size, but because he seemed so swollen with a sense of his own importance as to convey the idea that he was cramped for space—very much like an owl in the cage of a canary.

"Good morning, Squire Leech," said the widow.

"Good morning, ma'am. I apprehend you know my errand."

"I suppose you come for the interest, Squire Leech."

"You are quite right. Of course you are prepared to pay it."

Though the squire said "of course," he by no means expected that it would be ready, nor, for reasons which we know, did he desire it. He was rather discomfited, therefore, when Mrs. Carter said: "Did you bring a receipt with you, squire?"

"A receipt in full?" queried the great man.

"Yes, sir."

"Are you prepared to pay the whole to-day?"

"Yes, sir."

This ought to have been gratifying intelligence, but it was not. The squire looked quite crestfallen.

"No, I didn't bring a receipt," he said, slowly.

"I'll bring writing materials," said Herbert, promptly. He left the room, but appeared almost instantly with pen, ink, and paper.

The squire sat down to the table with a disappointed air, and slowly wrote the required document.

"He seems sorry to receive the money," thought Herbert, who was quick in reading the faces of others. "I wonder why?" and he gazed at the visitor in some perplexity.

The squire received the money, and handed the widow the receipt. Still he did not seem inclined to go. He was thinking how to broach the subject of selling the house.

"Mrs. Carter," he began, "forty-five dollars a year seems a good deal for you to pay."

"Yes, it is considerable," said the widow, surprised. Could it be that he intended to reduce the interest? That did not seem like him.

"For one in your circumstances I mean, of course. You've got to earn your own living, and your son's."

"Herbert does his share," said the mother. "When he is older I shall feel quite easy."

"But that time is a good way off. I've been thinking of your case, Mrs. Carter, and as a man of business I see my way clear to offer you a little advice."

"I shall be thankful for any advice, squire," said the widow, meekly. "Of course your judgment in business matters is much better than mine."

Herbert listened to this conversation with eager interest. What could the squire mean to advise?

"I've been thinking," said the squire, deliberately, "that it would be a good plan for you to sell this house."

"To sell it!" repeated Mrs. Carter, in surprise. "But where could I live?"

"You might hire a couple of rooms for yourself and Herbert."

Squire Leech is Baffled

"I don't see how mother would gain anything," interrupted Herbert. "She would have to pay rent."

"Very true, but she would get some money down for the house, over and above the mortgage."

"I don't know as anybody would want to buy it," said Mrs. Carter.

"I would take it off your hands, simply to oblige you," said the squire, with an air of extraordinary consideration. "I don't know that it would be of any particular use to me. I might not get a tenant. Still, I am better able to take the risk than you are to keep it."

"How much would you be willing to pay for it?" asked Herbert, who somehow suspected that the squire was more selfish than benevolent in the plan he had broached.

"Why," said Squire Leech, assuming a meditative look, "over and above the mortgage, I would be willing to pay three hundred dollars cash."

"That would make the value of the place only ten hundred and fifty dollars," said Herbert.

"Well, you don't consider it worth any more than that, do you?"

"My husband considered it worth fifteen hundred dollars," said the widow. "It cost him that."

The squire laughed heartily. "Really, my dear madam, that is utterly preposterous. Fifteen hundred dollars! Why, that is ridiculous."

"It cost that," said Herbert, sturdily.

"I very much doubt it," said the squire. "I don't believe it cost a cent over twelve hundred dollars."

"I have my husband's papers to show that it cost fifteen hundred," said the widow.

"Then all I have to say is, he was outrageously cheated," said the squire. "I believe I know as much about real estate as any man in town," he proceeded, pompously. "Indeed, I own more than any other man. I assure you, on my word, I have offered you a very good price."

"I would rather not sell," said the widow, gently, but decidedly.

"I will increase my offer to eleven hundred, including the mortgage," said the squire, who saw the prize slipping through his fingers, and felt it necessary to bid higher. "Eleven hundred dollars. That's three hundred and fifty dollars cash!"

"Mother, I am sure you won't think of selling for any such sum," expostulated Herbert.

"No," said his mother, "I don't want to sell."

"You stand very much in your own light, ma'am," said the squire, impatiently; "and you, Herbert, are too young to offer any advice on such a subject."

"I don't see why," said Herbert, independently. "I ought to feel interested in such a matter."

"You are a boy, and have no judgment. Boys of your age should be seen and not heard," said the squire, sternly.

"I can see what is best for my mother's interest," said Herbert.

"I decline to discuss the matter with you. I consider your interference impertinent," said the squire, becoming angry.

"Oh, Herbert!" said his mother, who was a little in awe of the great man of the village, "be respectful to Squire Leech."

"I mean to be," said Herbert, "but I'm sure he's wrong in thinking I have nothing to do with this matter."

"Reflect again, Mrs. Carter," persisted the squire, "of the advantages of my proposal. Think how comfortable you would feel in knowing that you had three hundred and fifty dollars on interest in the savings bank. I admit that I may not offer you quite as much as the place cost, but houses never fetch their first cost. I've made you a very fair offer, ma'am, very fair."

"I won't say anything as to that, Squire Leech, but this

house my poor husband built—in this house I have passed many happy years—and while we can keep it, Herbert and I, we will. There is no other place in town that would seem so much like home."

"This is all very sentimental, ma'am; but, permit me to say, very ridiculous," said the impatient squire, rising to go. "I'll give you time to think over what I have said, and I'll call again."

"I'll have that place yet," he muttered to himself, as he left the cottage. "I won't be balked by an obstinate woman and an impertinent boy."

CHAPTER XI

SICKNESS

SQUIRE LEECH was reluctant to give up his intended purchase. He had an idea that Herbert stood in the way, and he contrived to call upon the widow in the course of the following week, at a time when he knew our hero was away from home.

But he failed again.

"I'm very sorry to go contrary to your advice, Squire Leech," said Mrs. Carter, deprecatingly, "but I can't give up my home. Herbert, too, would be very much disappointed."

"I hope you will not allow yourself to be guided by the judgment of an inexperienced boy, ma'am," said the squire, mortified.

"I think I ought to consult my boy's wishes," said the widow.

"He doesn't know what is best for him."

"Perhaps not; but I feel with him at present. I'm sorry to disappoint you, Squire Leech."

"As to that, ma'am, I have no interest in the matter. I was only advising you for your good."

"I'm sure I'm much obliged to you."

"In fact, as your means are limited, I will stretch a point, and offer you fifty dollars more. I shouldn't be at all sure of getting my money back."

"Thank you; but I think we'll keep the house for the present. If I should find we couldn't afford it, I will let you know."

"I don't agree to keep to my offer after this week. 'Now or never' is my motto. I can draw the papers right out."

The widow shook her head, and reiterated in gentle tones her refusal. Squire Leech was provoked, and did not hide his feeling. As he only proposed to take the house to oblige her, as he represented, Mrs. Carter was surprised at his display of feeling. She was not a shrewd woman, and it did not occur to her that he had any selfish object in view in his advice.

"I didn't succeed, Mr. Banks," said the squire to his superintendent. "That Carter woman is dreadfully obstinate. Between ourselves, I judge it's her son that influences her."

"I think I have seen him—a boy of fourteen or fifteen."

"Yes, he's a very self-willed boy."

"You said you thought you would be able to foreclose, on account of their failing to pay the interest."

"They paid it. I was surprised at their promptness, till I learned from my son that they had received a legacy of a hundred dollars or so from a relative."

"That won't last always."

"No, the time will come when I can get the place on my own terms. I am determined to have it."

"Then Brown will have to find a different house."

"Yes; I have heard of an old house that will do temporarily, till I get the widow Carter's. It's a little out of

Sickness

the village, and is in rather a dilapidated condition, but it will do for a few months or a year, and that will fetch round the Carters."

The house referred to was secured, and the superintendent's cousin moved to Wrayburn. But neither the squire nor Mr. Banks forgave Herbert for his assumed instrumentality in thwarting their plans.

The next winter Mrs. Carter was unfortunate enough to be laid up with severe sickness from December to March. Herbert devoted himself to her comfort, and performed nearly all his mother's customary work. Washing and ironing, however, he was obliged to have done. When the sickness commenced, the hundred dollars left by his uncle was unbroken, but for three months neither he nor, of course, his mother, was able to earn anything of any amount, while their expenses were necessarily increased.

At the opening of April, Herbert had the satisfaction of seeing his mother, fully recovered, assume her usual place in the little household. This was pleasant, but there was a drawback to his satisfaction. The legacy had dwindled to twenty-five dollars.

He reported this to his mother.

"How unlucky that I should have been sick so long!" said Mrs. Carter, sighing.

"How lucky we had the legacy to fall back upon!" said Herbert.

"I don't know how we could have got along without that, truly."

"Mother, I must look about for work. I ought to be earning four or five dollars a week at my age."

"You are only fifteen."

"But I am stout and strong of my age. I shall soon be a man. Don't you see my mustache coming, mother?" said Herbert, with a laugh.

"Not very distinctly; but perhaps my eyesight is growing poor," answered his mother, smiling.

"The trouble is," said Herbert, thoughtfully, "there is very little chance of work in this town."

"I wonder whether Squire Leech wouldn't hire you through the spring and summer on one of his farms. I heard that he is going to hire a boy."

"I am not sure whether he would be willing to hire me, however much he wanted a boy."

"Why not?"

"He don't seem to like me, nor does Mr. Banks like me."

"What can they have against you? I thought everybody liked you."

"That's because you are my mother, but the squire doesn't feel maternal so far as I am concerned. I didn't understand it at first, but now I do."

"What is it?"

"You remember the squire tried hard to get you to sell this place."

"That was last year."

"And you wouldn't sell. That is why he is angry with both of us."

"But I don't understand why he should be," said the widow, innocently. "He said he would take it only as a favor to me."

"That was all 'gammon.' Excuse the word, which isn't very elegant, I admit, but it's the right word for all that. The squire wanted the place very much."

"What could he do with it? He couldn't live in it himself."

"Not much. I can imagine the look of disgust James's face would wear at the idea of such a thing. He wanted it for Nahum Brown, who lives in the old house up the road. You know Brown, who is a cousin of Mr. Banks, the superintendent, and he is very anxious to get hold of our house."

"How did you learn all this, Herbert? I never knew it before."

Sickness

"Tom Banks let it out one day."

"I don't see how the squire can dislike us for wanting to stay in our old home."

"There are a good many things you don't understand —about selfish men—mother. That is why I am afraid it won't be much use to ask the squire for employment."

"You may be mistaken about his feelings, Herbert."

"At any rate, I'll go to him, if I can't find employment anywhere else in the village."

"I wish you would, that is, if you don't think farm work will be too hard for you."

"I'll risk that."

In pursuance of this promise, Herbert, after ascertaining that there was no work to be had anywhere else in the village, called one fine morning at the imposing residence of Squire Leech.

James was in the yard, at work on a kite.

"Have you come to see me?" said James, superciliously.

"No; I wanted to see your father."

"What about?"

Herbert was about to answer "on business," but it occurred to him that it would be better policy to keep on friendly terms with James, and he said: "I am looking for work, and I thought he might have some for me."

"Perhaps so," said James, patronizingly. "Of course, one in your position must work for a living."

"Don't you expect to work?" asked Herbert, in some curiosity.

"Not with my hands, of course," said James. "I may study some genteel profession, such as law."

"I am too poor to be genteel," said Herbert, amused.

"Of course. You will probably be a day laborer."

"I hope to rise to something better in time," said Herbert. "For the present I shall be glad to work by the day, or the month, if your father will engage me."

"I think my father is at home; you can ring and see,"

said James, who could be kind to one who was willing to acknowledge his inferiority.

Herbert rang the bell, and was ushered into the presence of Squire Leech, who was examining some papers in the back parlor.

CHAPTER XII

"POOR AND PROUD"

"Good morning, Squire Leech," said Herbert, politely.

"Good morning," said the squire, jumping to the conclusion that the Carters had made up their minds to sell their place. "Do you wish to see me?"

"Yes, sir; I hope I don't interrupt you."

"Go on," said the squire, waving his hand. "I am busy, to be sure, but I can give you a few minutes."

He resolved to take advantage of Mrs. Carter's necessities, and make a smaller offer for the place. In this way he would make her suffer for her former obstinate refusal to entertain his proposition.

His face fell when Herbert said: "I came to ask you if you could give me employment on one of your farms. My mother has been sick, and I feel that I ought to be doing something to earn money."

"Ahem!" said the squire, "I leave all such matters to Mr. Banks. Was that all you wished to say to me?"

"I believe so," said Herbert. "Will there be any use in applying to Mr. Banks?"

"I don't know whether he has got help enough or not. Your mother has been sick, hasn't she?"

"Yes, sir; all winter."

"I heard of it. I suppose you found it expensive, eh?"

"Yes, sir. Neither of us could earn anything."

"You are in debt, then?"

"No, sir. My uncle left us some money last year. That kept us along."

"It's pretty much used up now, I suppose?"

"Not quite."

Herbert was inclined to be surprised at the squire's apparent interest in their affairs, but the motive soon became apparent.

"Well, you have made up your mind to sell the house now, I suppose?" said the squire.

"No, we hadn't thought of it."

"But you'll have to."

"Not if I can get employment," said Herbert. "Our expenses are very small, and we can live on a little."

The great man frowned.

"That is all nonsense," he said, impatiently. "It is quite impossible for you to hold on to the house. I am willing to give you cash down three hundred dollars over and above the mortgage for it."

"That isn't as much as you offered last year," said Herbert, shrewdly.

"I believe I did offer three hundred and fifty then."

"Your last offer was fifty dollars more than that."

"It may be so, but I told your mother that it wasn't a standing offer. She must accept it then or not at all."

"We don't ask you to purchase," said Herbert, independently. "I had no idea of such a thing when I came here."

"That makes no difference. You will have to sell, of course, and I have made up my mind to offer you three hundred and fifty. If you had taken me up at the time, I would have given you fifty more. You can't expect that now, however."

"We don't expect anything. The house is not for sale."

"Then, why are you taking up my valuable time?" demanded the squire, frowning with displeasure.

"I beg your pardon, sir. I only came in to ask for employment."

"That I might have given you, if you hadn't been so unreasonable."

"I don't think we are unreasonable, Squire Leech. Even if we were willing to sell, we should ask, at least, fourteen hundred dollars for the place."

"Fourteen hundred! Are you crazy? I never heard of such a thing."

"The place, land and all, cost my father fifteen hundred."

"I don't believe it."

"We've got his papers to show that it is so."

"It isn't worth near that now."

"It is certainly worth more than eleven hundred, which is all you offer."

"Look here, Carter," said the squire, "I don't mind telling you that I want the place for one of my men—Brown. That is my only object in making you an offer at all. He is the cousin of Mr. Banks, my superintendent, and I rather think Banks will find you something to do, if you will induce your mother to sell the place."

"I can't do that," said Herbert, slowly. "I can't consent to my mother making such a sacrifice. She might as well give you three or four hundred dollars as sell the place so much under price."

"You are a boy, and know nothing about business. You think property must necessarily bring its first cost, though, mind you, I don't admit that yours cost anything like fifteen hundred dollars."

"I am inexperienced," Herbert admitted, "but I am sure it would be foolish to sell for eleven hundred dollars."

"You may have to sell for less."

"How is that?"

"If you are not prepared with the interest when the time comes, I shall foreclose."

"You wouldn't be so hard on us as that, Squire Leech," said Herbert, anxiously.

"I don't call it hard, it is only just and legal. When that time comes, I don't promise to pay as much as I offer to-day."

Herbert looked serious. He saw that the squire meant just what he said; that, in fact, he was lying in wait till their need should put them in his power.

"Well," said the squire, triumphantly, "you see how the matter stands now?"

"I do," said Herbert.

"Then you will cease your foolish opposition to what is best for you."

"I will speak to my mother about it," said Herbert, rising. "The place is hers, not mine, and she must decide."

"Without your offering any foolish advice, I hope."

"I can't say as to that, Squire Leech. I will bid you good morning."

"Good morning. If you change your mind, call again, and we will see about the employment."

"Well," said James, as Herbert came out, "did you get work?"

"Not yet; your father is not sure whether he will have any for me."

"When I am a man," said James, pompously, "I dare say I may be able to throw something in your way."

"Thank you," said Herbert, tempted to smile in spite of his serious thoughts.

"I shall be richer than my father," added James, "as his property is increasing every year."

"You have an excellent prospect before you," said Herbert, half enviously.

"That's so. Wouldn't you like to change places with me?"

"I am not sure about that."

"You are not sure about that?" repeated James, incredulously.

"No."

"Why, I am a rich man's son."

"I know that; but I have an excellent mother."

"She has got no money."

"I should not value her more if she were worth a million," said Herbert, warmly.

"Of course," said James; "but that won't save you from being a day laborer."

"It is my great ambition just at present to become a day laborer," said Herbert, smiling.

"Of course, there's a great difference between us. But I say, Carter, can you help me with this kite? There's something wrong about it. It won't fly."

Herbert looked at it critically.

"The trouble is with the frame," he said. "It's too heavy."

"I wish you'd help me about it."

Very good-naturedly our hero set to work, and in the course of twenty minutes or so the difficulty was obviated. The kite would fly.

"You may stay and help me fly it," said James, condescendingly.

"Thank you; I shall be needed at home."

"Oh, I forgot. Your time is valuable. Here, take this."

James, with extraordinary liberality, held out five cents to Herbert.

"What is that for?" asked Herbert, puzzled, and not offering to take the money.

"For your help about the kite."

"Oh, I wouldn't think of charging anything for that," said Herbert, amused.

"Why not? You are poor, and I am rich."

"I know it, but I don't want money for a trifle like that."

"Just as you say," said James, returning the money to his pocket, a little relieved, if the truth must be told, that the coin was not accepted, for he was naturally fond of money.

"Good morning," said Herbert, turning to go. "If the kite gets out of order, you can call upon me any time."

"I wonder why he didn't take the money," thought James. "He may be poor and proud; I've heard of such cases; but of course it would be absurd for a boy in his position to be proud."

Herbert kept on his way with a very serious face. It seemed as if they must lose their home, after all.

CHAPTER XIII

MR. BANKS, THE SUPERINTENDENT

AFTER his interview with Squire Leech, Herbert walked home slowly and thoughtfully. He comprehended now all the danger of the situation. The squire wanted their house, and was mean enough to desire to get it at less than its value, though two or three hundred dollars would have been of little account to him, while to the poor widow whom he wished to defraud it was a great sum.

"How can a rich man be so mean?" exclaimed Herbert, indignantly.

That question has puzzled more than our hero. Is there something in riches that dwarfs the man, and makes him mean and ignoble? In too many instances such appears to be the effect.

"Well, mother," said Herbert, when he returned to the cottage, "I've been to see Squire Leech."

"What success did you meet with?" asked his mother, anxiously.

"He will probably give me employment."

"You see, Herbert, you misjudged him, after all," said the widow, her face brightening.

"Wait and see if I did. There is a condition attached."

"What is that?"

"That you will sell him the cottage."

"Did he mention that?"

"Yes, he offered three hundred dollars over and above the mortgage."

"Why, he offered more than that last year."

"I reminded him of that."

"What did he say?"

"He said he would have given three hundred and fifty if we hadn't been so unreasonable as to refuse then. Now, as you have been sick, he expects he can get the place on his own terms."

"I didn't think Squire Leech would be so ungenerous."

"He hinted, besides, that when the next interest is due, he would foreclose, if the money were not ready."

"It won't be ready, I am afraid, Herbert," said his mother, depressed. "What shall we do? I am afraid we shall be forced to sell the place, though it would be hard to leave it."

"There's a month before the interest comes due, mother," said Herbert, with energy. "Something may turn up."

But his mother was not so hopeful as he.

"What can turn up?" she said.

"I may get employment."

"Even if you do, a boy can earn little in the country."

"That is true, mother, but somehow I feel hopeful."

"That is because you are young, Herbert. It is natural for youth to be hopeful."

"Well, mother, isn't it better to be hopeful than despondent?"

"But it won't alter wants."

"Suppose the worst to happen—suppose we do leave the house—we shall have three hundred or three hundred and fifty dollars in cash, to keep us from starving."

Mr. Banks, the Superintendent 61

"And when that is gone?"

"Before that is gone, I shall be earning good wages somewhere. You see, mother, matters are not as bad as they might be, after all."

In spite of her doubts, Mrs. Carter was cheered by her son's hopeful tone.

"Perhaps you are right," she said. "Since God orders all things, we ought not to be discouraged."

"Now you are sensible, mother. How much money have you got left?"

"Twenty-five dollars."

"Why, that's enough to pay the interest, and a little over."

"But how are we to live for the next month?"

"I ought to earn money enough for that."

"If there were any chance of finding work."

"Well, I will go out again to-morrow."

Herbert spoke with a confidence which he did not feel. Wrayburn was not a large village, and, in general, boys were to be found in families where a boy's work was required. In fact, the only one who seemed likely to have work for a boy was Mr. Banks, the squire's farm superintendent. His son, Tom, might indeed have worked, had he been inclined; but he was naturally indolent, and his father was too indulgent to compel him to work. He was an only child, and bade fair to be spoiled. Though only fifteen, he had already learned to smoke and drink, and the only limit to either was his scanty pocket money.

As Herbert was walking up the street in perplexity, he fell in with Tom, who was smoking a cheap cigar with the air of an old smoker.

"Where are you bound, Herbert?" he asked.

"Nowhere in particular. I wish I knew where to go."

"Come fishing with me."

"I haven't time."

"You said you were not going anywhere in particular."

"Because I don't know where to go."

"Then, why not go with me?"

"I want to find work somewhere."

Tom shrugged his shoulders.

"That's just what I am not anxious to find," he said. "My father keeps thinking every day that I ought to be at work, but I don't see it."

Tom winked here, and looked, or thought he looked, uncommonly sly.

"Then, your father has work for a boy to do," said Herbert, getting interested.

"Oh, yes, it is spring now, and the busy season is beginning. But that sort of work don't suit me. I will never be a farmer. When I get a little older, I should like to go to the city, and enter a store. That would be jolly."

"You might get tired of it."

"No, I wouldn't; I'm sick of this stupid old town, though. There's nothing going on."

"I say, Tom, as you don't want to work, do you think your father would give me a chance?"

"I don't know," said Tom. "I'll speak to him if you want me to."

"I wish you would."

"There'll be one advantage about it. If he hires you, he won't be at me to work all the time. I'll do it. Come along, and I'll speak to him now."

"Thank you, Tom."

"Oh, you needn't thank me. It's for my own sake I'm doing it as much as yours," said Tom, who was at least frank in his selfishness.

They went to the small house occupied, much against his will, by Amos Banks. He was in the field, with one of his men, when Tom and Herbert came up, and, jumping over the stone wall, approached him.

"Well, Tom," said his father, "you have come just in time. I want you to ride the horse to plow."

"I can't, father; I don't feel well to-day."

"What's the matter?"

"Oh, I've got a headache."

"Riding will do you good."

"No, it won't," said Tom, confidently; "but if you want a boy to help you, here he is."

Mr. Banks turned to Herbert.

"You are Herbert Carter," he said.

"Yes, sir. I would like very much to get a chance to work."

"You're the widow Carter's son?"

"Yes, sir."

"Has your mother decided to sell her cottage?"

"I don't think she has, Mr. Banks."

"Of course you know that Squire Leech wants to buy it."

"Yes, sir. He told me that he wanted to purchase it for your use."

"Just so," said the superintendent, stopping work; "I've taken a fancy to that house, and so has Mrs. Banks. You had better accept the squire's offer."

"That would be too much of a sacrifice, Mr. Banks. The squire wants to get the place considerably below its value."

"Very likely you overvalue it."

"Mother is attached to it. She would rather have it than a nicer house. Father built it, and it was here they lived for nearly fifteen years."

"No doubt—no doubt," said Banks, impatiently; "but poor folks can't afford to be sentimental. If it's for your mother's interest to sell, then she'd ought to sell, that's my opinion."

"We may have to sell some time, but as long as we can hold on to the place, we mean to."

"I may as well say," said the superintendent, "that the squire has authorized me to hire you to work, in case your mother consents to sell."

"Is that the condition?"

"Yes."

"Then," said Herbert, turning away, "I am afraid I must give up the chance."

"That's an obstinate boy," said Banks, looking after him; "but he'll come around after a while. The squire says he'll have to, or be turned out for not paying the interest."

CHAPTER XIV

HERBERT'S NEW UNDERTAKING

To be willing to work, and yet to be unable to find an opportunity, was certainly a hardship. Herbert was a boy of active temperament, and, even had he not needed the wages of labor, he would still have felt it necessary to his happiness to do something.

In the course of his walks about the village, he stopped at the house of a carpenter, who bore the rather peculiar name of Jeremiah Crane. Mr. Crane owned about an acre and a half of land, which might have been cultivated, but at the time Herbert called, early in April, there were no indications of this intention. The carpenter was at work in a small shop just beyond the house, and there Herbert found him.

"Well, Herbert," said Mr. Crane, in a friendly manner, "what are you up to nowadays?"

"Nothing profitable, Mr. Crane; I am wandering about in search of work."

"Can't you find any?"

"Not yet."

"Have you been to Squire Leech?"

Herbert's New Undertaking

"Yes."

"I should think he might find something for you to do."

"There is a little difficulty in the way."

"What is that?"

Then Herbert told Mr. Crane about the squire's wish to purchase their cottage, and his vexation because they were not willing to sell.

"Seems to me that's unreasonable in the squire. He acts as if it was your duty to oblige him."

"I don't know but we shall have to come to his terms," said Herbert, rather dejectedly. "We certainly shall if I don't find anything to do."

"I wish I could help you; but, if you were to learn my trade, you wouldn't be worth any wages for nigh a year, and you couldn't afford to work so long without pay."

"No, I couldn't."

"Besides, in a village like this, there isn't more than enough work for one man. Why, there isn't more than one new house built a year. If the squire wants to provide Mr. Banks with a house, why doesn't he build him one? He might just as well as not."

"It would cost him more than to buy our place at the price he offers."

"So it would. Your place must have cost fifteen hundred dollars, land and all."

"So I did, but the squire laughed at the idea. All he offers is eleven hundred."

"Don't you sell at that price. It would be too much of a sacrifice."

"We won't unless we are obliged to."

"I hope you won't be obliged to. A man as rich as Squire Leech ought not to try to get it under price."

"I suppose he wants to make a good bargain, no matter if it is at our expense. I wish you had a farm, Mr. Crane, so you could give me work on it."

"I've got more farm now than I can take care of."

"Don't you have a garden?"

"I've got the land, but no time to work on it. My wife often wishes we had our own vegetables, instead of having to buy, but you see, after working in the shop, or outside, all day, I'm too tired to work on land."

"How much land have you?"

"About an acre that I could cultivate, I suppose."

"Engage me to take care of it. I'll do all the work, and your wife can have her own vegetables."

"Really, I never thought of that," said the carpenter. "I don't know but it might be a good idea. How much pay would you want?"

"I'll tell you," said Herbert, who had a business turn, and who had already matured the plan in his own mind. "If you will pay for plowing, and provide seed, I will do the planting, and gather it when harvest time comes, for one-third of the crop."

"You mean, you will take your pay in vegetables?"

"Yes," said Herbert, promptly. "If there is more than you need, I can sell the surplus. What do you say?"

"It strikes me as a fair offer, Herbert. Just wait a minute, and I'll go and ask my wife what she thinks of it."

Mr. Crane went into the house, leaving Herbert in the shop. He reappeared in five minutes. Herbert, to whom the plan seemed every minute more desirable, awaited his report eagerly.

"My wife is all for your plan," he said. "She says it is the only way she knows of likely to give her the fresh vegetables she wants. Besides, she thinks well of you. So, it's a settled thing, if you say so."

"I do say so," Herbert replied, promptly.

"Now, when will you have it plowed?"

"I shall leave all that to you. I haven't time to make arrangements. You can engage anybody you like to do the plowing, and I will pay the bill."

"Then, as to the seed?"

Herbert's New Undertaking

"There, again, I trust all to you. You can buy what you find to be necessary, and the bill may be sent to me. You may ask Mrs. Crane what vegetables she wants."

"All right," said Herbert.

"Please understand," said the carpenter, "that I will do what I have said, but I don't want to be worried about the details. You are a boy, but I shall trust to your judgment, as you are interested in the result."

"Thank you," said Herbert, rather proud of the confidence reposed in him. "I will do what I can to justify your confidence. I'll go right off and see about the plowing."

"Very well."

Whatever Herbert did was done promptly. He knew of a man named Kimball, a farmer on a small scale, who was accustomed to do work for neighbors, not having enough work of his own to occupy his whole time. He went to see him at once.

"Mr. Kimball," he said, "I want to know if I can engage you to do some plowing for me."

"For you!" repeated the farmer, opening his eyes. "Why, you haven't taken a farm, have you?"

"Not yet," said Herbert, smiling; "but I've agreed to cultivate a little land on shares."

"Sho! you don't say so! What land is it?"

"It's the field behind Mr. Crane's house."

"So he's engaged you, has he? Well, I've often wondered why he didn't cultivate it. Might as well as not."

"It's my idea. I proposed it to him. Now, when can you come?"

"Wait a minute," said the farmer, cautiously; "who's a-going to pay me?"

"Mr. Crane. He told me to engage somebody, and he would pay the bill."

"That's all right, then," said the farmer, in a tone of satisfaction; "Crane's a man that always pays his bills."

"I hope I shall have the same reputation," said Herbert.

"I hope you will, but you're only a boy, you know, and I couldn't collect of a minor. That's the law."

"I shouldn't think anybody'd be dishonest enough to bring that as an excuse."

"Plenty would do it, so I have to be careful. What time do you want me to do the work for you?"

"As soon as you can."

"Let me see, I guess I can come to-morrow. There ain't anything very pressing for me to do then."

"That's good," said Herbert, with satisfaction. "You'll find me there, and I can ride the horse to plow if you want me to."

"I should like to have you."

"Well, thought Herbert, as he started for home to tell his mother what he had done, "I've made a beginning."

"I suppose you haven't found any work yet, Herbert," said his mother, in a tone of resignation, as he entered the little cottage.

"Yes, I have; though I shall have to wait some time for the pay."

"What is it, Herbert?"

"I'm going to cultivate a garden on shares, mother; so next fall and winter you can have all the vegetables you want."

"How is that, Herbert? Tell me all about it."

When Herbert had detailed the contract he had entered into, he was glad to find that his mother approved of it. She declared that it would be very satisfactory to her to have an abundant stock of vegetables, but she said, doubtfully: "Do you think you know enough of farming to attend to all the work?"

"If I don't I can easily ask some farmer," said Herbert, confidently. "I am not in the least afraid to undertake the job."

He went to bed that night feeling that at last he had obtained something to do.

The reader will perhaps recall the statement in our first chapter that there was a little land connected with the cottage, which was used for the growth of vegetables. This, in fact, supplied nearly all that was required by the widow and her son, and the probability was that Herbert would be able to send to market nearly all his share of vegetables obtained under his new contract, and thus obtain payment in money, of which they were so much in need.

CHAPTER XV

THE CRISIS APPROACHES

HERBERT went to work in earnest. It took only part of one day to plow the field which he was to cultivate. He decided, after consultation with Mrs. Crane, to appropriate two-thirds of the land to potatoes, and the remainder to different kinds of vegetables. He was guided partly by the consideration of which would be most marketable.

On the third day, while at work, he heard his name called. It must be explained that Mr. Crane's house and land were on the corner of two streets, so that he was in full sight, while in the field, from the side street. Looking up, he recognized James Leech, who was surveying him with evident curiosity.

"Good morning, James," said Herbert, going on with his work.

"I see you've got a job," said James.

"Yes."

"Has Mr. Crane hired you?"

"Not exactly."

"Then, why are you at work in his field?"

"Because I've agreed to work it on shares."

"How is that?"

"I am to have a third of the crops to pay me for my services."

"What can you do with it?"

"Part of the vegetables we can use at home, and the balance I shall sell."

"I shouldn't think you'd like that arrangement."

"Why not?"

"Because you have so long to wait for your pay."

"That is true, but it's better than not working at all, and I've tried all over the village in vain to get employment."

"Do you think you'll make much out of it?"

"I don't think I shall make my fortune, but I shall make something."

"Don't it tire you to work?" asked James, with some curiosity.

"Of course, if I work all day; but I don't mind that."

"I should."

"You are not used to work."

"I should say not," returned James, with pride. "I never worked in my life."

It was a strange thing to be proud of, but there are some who have nothing better to be proud of.

"I like to work," said Herbert.

"You do?"

"Yes, only I like to get something for my labor. You expect to work some time, don't you?"

"Not with my hands," said James. "I shall never be reduced to that."

"Do you think it so very bad to work with your hands? Isn't it respectable?"

"Oh, I suppose it's respectable," said James; "but only the lower classes do it."

"Am I one of the lower classes?" asked Herbert, amused.

The Crisis Approaches

"Of course you are."

"But suppose I should get rich some day," said Herbert.

"That isn't very likely. You can't get rich raising vegetables."

"No, I don't expect to. Still, I may in some other way. Didn't you ever know any poor boys that got rich?"

"I suppose there have been some," admitted James.

"Haven't you ever heard of Vanderbilt?"

"Of course I have. Father says he's worth forty millions."

"Don't you consider him a gentleman?"

"Of course I do."

"Well, he was a poor boy once, and used to ferry passengers across from Staten Island to New York."

"Did he? I didn't know that."

"Suppose my uncle had left me all his fortune—a hundred thousand dollars—would I have been a gentleman, then?"

"Yes, but it isn't the same as if you had always been rich."

"I don't agree with your ideas, James. It seems to me something besides money is needed to make a gentleman; still, I hope to get on in the world, and I shouldn't object to being rich, though I don't see any prospect of it just at present."

"No," said James. "You will probably always be poor."

"That's very encouraging," said Herbert, laughing. "How about yourself?"

"Oh, I shall be a rich man like father."

"That's very encouraging for you. I hope when you are a man you'll give me work if I need it."

"I will bear it in mind," said James, with an important air. "Now I must be going."

That day, at dinner, James said to his father: "That Carter boy has got a job."

"Has he?" asked the squire, not very well pleased.

"Yes, he's working at Mr. Crane's."

"What is he doing?"

"Working in the garden."

"What wages does Crane pay him?"

"None at all. He says he has agreed to work for the third of the crops."

"Did he say that?" asked the squire, with satisfaction.

"Yes, he told me so this morning."

"You are sure he gets no money?"

"Yes; he is paid wholly in vegetables. He said he couldn't find employment anywhere else in the village, so he had to work that way."

"That boy stands very much in his own light," said the squire.

"How is that, father?"

"I told him Mr. Banks would give him work if he would agree to sell me his cottage."

"He doesn't own it, does he?"

"His mother, of course, I mean. It's the boy that keeps her from selling it."

"Why does he do that?"

"Oh, they've got a silly notion that no other place would seem like home to them, and, besides, they think I don't offer them enough."

"How much do you offer them?"

"Eleven hundred dollars; that is, I have a mortgage on the place for seven hundred and fifty. I offer them three hundred and fifty dollars besides."

"Is that all the money they are worth?"

"Yes; they are very foolish to refuse, for they'll have to come to it some time. In about a week the interest comes due, and I'm very sure they won't be able to meet it."

"Suppose they don't?"

"Then," said the squire, with a satisfied smile, "I shall take possession, and they'll have to sell."

The Crisis Approaches

"Herbert says he hopes to be rich some time."

"I dare say," said the squire, laughing heartily. "Everybody does, so far as I know."

"Do you think there is any chance of it?"

"About one in a thousand."

"I shouldn't want the lower classes to get rich," said James, thoughtfully. "They'd think they were our equals."

"Yes, no doubt."

James was not aware that his grandfather had once been a poor mechanic, or rather he ignored it. He chose to consider that he had sprung from a long line of wealthy ancestors. His father heard with pleasure that Herbert was not likely to realize any money at present for his services. Already he felt that the little cottage was as good as his. It was only a week now to the time of paying interest, and he was very sure that Mrs. Carter would be unprepared to meet it.

"In that case," he decided, "I will certainly foreclose. There will be no sense in granting them any further indulgence. It will be for their interest to sell the cottage, and get rid of the burden which the interest imposes. Really, they ought to consider it a favor that I am willing to take it off their hands."

We are very apt to think it is for the interest of others to do what we greatly desire, and I don't suppose the squire was singular in this. I think, however, that there are many who are less selfish and more considerate of others.

Herbert, too, was thinking, and thinking seriously, of the interest that was so soon coming due. In spite of his own and his mother's economy, when the preceding day arrived, all they could raise toward the payment was thirteen dollars, and the sum required was twenty-two dollars and a half.

"Mother," said Herbert, at dinner the day before, "I

see only one chance for us, and that is, to borrow the money. If anyone would lend us ten dollars we could pay the interest, and then we should be free from anxiety for six months."

"I am afraid you will find that difficult," said his mother. "The squire is the only rich man in the village, and of course we can't apply to him."

"At any rate, I can but try. Instead of going to work this afternoon, I shall go about and try to borrow the money. If I can't, then I suppose we must give up the house."

Certainly the prospect seemed far from cheerful.

CHAPTER XVI

AN UNEXPECTED OFFER

It was with very little confidence in his ultimate success that Herbert set out on his borrowing expedition. The number of those who could be called capitalists in a small village like Wrayburn was very small, and it happened very remarkably that all of them were short of funds. One man had just bought a yoke of oxen, and so spent all his available cash; another had been shingling his barn; and still another confessed to having money, but it was in the savings bank, and he didn't like to disturb it.

So, at supper time, Herbert came in, depressed and dispirited.

"Well, mother, it's no use," he said, as her anxious look met his.

"I didn't much think you could borrow the money," she answered, trying to look cheerful.

"There's only one thing remains to be done," said Herbert.

"What is that?"

An Unexpected Offer

"To try to induce the squire to give us more time."

"I don't think he will do that."

"Nor I. In that case we must come to his terms; but it's a pity to sacrifice the property, mother."

"Yes, Herbert; I shall be sorry to leave the old place," she sighed. "You were born here, and your father was always very much attached to it. But poor folks can't have everything they wish, and it might be worse."

"Yes, it might be worse, and if the squire was not so bent in getting the place into his hands, it might be better."

"I suppose we ought not to blame him for looking out for his own interest."

"Yes, we ought; when it seems that he is ready to injure his poorer neighbors."

Mrs. Carter did not reply. She did not wish further to incense her son against the squire, yet in her heart she could not help agreeing with him.

The next day Herbert did not go to work as usual. He did not feel like it, while matters were in such uncertainty. He knew the squire would be at the cottage a little before twelve o'clock, and he wanted to be with his mother at that time, for he felt that, if the place must be sold, he would be more likely to get good terms for it than his mother, who was of an easy and yielding disposition.

He took a little walk in the course of the forenoon, not with any particular object in view, but in order to pass the time. As he was passing the hotel—for there was a small hotel in the village—he heard his name called. Turning round, he found that it was the landlord who had called him.

"Come here a minute, Herbert," he said.

Herbert obeyed the summons.

"What are you doing nowadays?" he asked.

"I have turned farmer," said our hero.

"Whom are you working for?"

"For myself."

"How is that? I don't understand."

"I am cultivating Mr. Crane's land on shares."

"Does it take up all your time?"

"No; I would only work part of the day if I had anything else to do."

"I'll tell you what I have been thinking of. There's a young man boarding with me from the city, a Mr. Cameron. He was a college student, but his eyes gave out, and the doctor sent him out of the city to get well. He wants some one to read to him part of the time, and go about with him for company. He is from a rich family—the son of a wealthy manufacturer—and he will be willing to pay a fair price."

"Do you think I would suit him?" asked Herbert, eagerly.

"Yes, I think you would. You are a good scholar, and when I mentioned you to him, he said he would like to see you. He said he would prefer a boy, as he would be more ready to adapt himself to his wishes."

"When can I see Mr. Cameron?" asked our hero.

"Come in now. You will find him in his room. Here, John, show Herbert up to number six."

Herbert was ushered into one of the best rooms the hotel afforded. A young man, of pleasant appearance, was sitting at the window, with a green shade over his eyes. He pushed up this, that he might see Herbert.

"This is Herbert Carter, Mr. Cameron," said John, unceremoniously.

"I am glad to see you, Herbert," said the young man, smiling as he extended his hand. He was secretly pleased with Herbert's open and manly face. "Did the landlord say why I might need your assistance?"

"He said your eyes were affected."

"Yes, they broke down a month since. I am a student of Yale College, in the junior class. I suppose I tasked

An Unexpected Offer

my eyes too severely. At any rate, they gave out, and I am forbidden to use them at all."

"That must be a great loss to you," said Herbert, with sympathy.

"It is. I am very fond of reading and study, and the time passes very heavily in the absence of my usual employment."

"I don't know what I should do if I could not use my eyes."

"You would find it a great hardship. Now I must tell you why I came here. The doctor told me I should be better off in the country than in the city. He said that the sight of the green grass would be good for me, and the fresh air, in improving my general health, would help my eyes also. I hadn't much choice as to a place, but some one mentioned Wrayburn, and so I came here. But I soon found that, unless I got some pleasant company and some one who could read to me, I should die of weariness. That brings me to my object in asking you to call upon me. How is your time occupied?"

"I have taken an acre of land to cultivate on shares," answered Herbert. "It was because I could find nothing else to do, and must do something."

"Does that keep you pretty busy?"

"It is planting time now, but I could get along with working there half a day."

"And could you place yourself at my disposal the other half?"

"I should be glad to do it," answered Herbert.

"Suppose, then, that you work in the field in the forenoon, and give me every afternoon."

"All right," said Herbert, promptly.

"Now comes another question. What pay would you expect for giving me so much of your time?"

"I shouldn't know what to charge, Mr. Cameron. I leave that matter entirely with you."

An Unexpected Offer

"Would you be satisfied with five dollars a week?"

Five dollars a week! Herbert could hardly believe his ears. Why, he would have been well paid if this had been given him for the whole of his time, but for half it seemed munificent.

"I am afraid I can't earn that much," he answered. "I would be willing to take less."

"You don't know how hard I shall make you work," said the young man, smiling. "I insist upon paying you five dollars a week."

"I don't seriously object," said Herbert, smiling; "but if you think, after the first week, that it is too much, you can pay me less."

"I see that we are not likely to quarrel on the subject of salary, then. When can you begin?"

"This afternoon, if you wish."

"I do wish it, otherwise the afternoon would pass very slowly to me."

"Then, I will be here at one o'clock."

"Half past one will do."

"I will be on hand. Till then I will bid you good morning, as I shall be wanted at home."

"Very well, Herbert."

Herbert left the room and hurried home, for it was nearly twelve. On the way he stopped at the post office, and found a letter addressed to his mother. He did not recognize the handwriting, nor, such was his hurry, did he notice where it was postmarked. He had no watch, but thought it must be close upon twelve o'clock. So he thrust the letter into his pocket, and continued his way homeward on a half run. He was in time, for, just as he reached the front gate from one direction, the squire reached it from the other.

"Good morning," said the squire, a little stiffly. "Is your mother at home?"

"I presume she is. Won't you come in?"

What the Letter Contained 79

"I wonder if they've got the money ready," thought the squire, as he followed Herbert into the modest sitting room.

CHAPTER XVII

WHAT THE LETTER CONTAINED

LEAVING the squire in the sitting room, Herbert went in quest of his mother.

"Squire Leech is here," he said.

"What shall we say to him?" asked his mother, soberly.

"Wait a minute and I will tell you," said Herbert, his face brightening.

"I've had a stroke of luck, mother. I've been engaged to work afternoons, at five dollars a week."

"Who has engaged to pay you such high wages?" asked Mrs. Carter, astonished.

"A young man staying at the hotel, whose eyes are weak. I am to read to him, and do whatever else he requires. I got the chance through the landlord."

"You are certainly fortunate," said his mother, gratified.

"Now, what I am going to propose to the squire is to wait two or three weeks for the balance of the interest till I can make it up out of my wages."

"If he weren't so anxious to get possession of the place he would; but I am afraid on that account he will refuse. But we ought to go in."

Mrs. Carter removed the apron which she had worn about her work, and entered the sitting room, followed by Herbert.

"I hope you will excuse my keeping you waiting, Squire Leech," she said.

"Certainly, ma'am, though I am rather in a hurry."

"I suppose you have come about the interest?"

"It is due to-day, as, of course, you know."

"Yes."

"I suppose you have it ready," said the squire, eyeing her shrewdly.

"I can pay you fifteen dollars of it," said the widow, nervously.

Squire Leech felt exultant, but he only frowned.

"It amounts to twenty-two dollars and a half," he said, sharply.

"I know that, and I shall be able to pay the remainder if you will be kind enough to wait two or three weeks."

Not knowing anything of Herbert's good fortune, Squire Leech utterly disbelieved this. He knew no source from which the widow could get the money.

"It is easy enough to make promises," he said, with a sneer, "but that doesn't satisfy me. I want my money."

Now Herbert felt it time for him to take part in the conversation.

"My mother can keep her promise," he said.

"Can she? Perhaps you will explain where you expect to get the money."

"From my wages," answered Herbert, proudly.

"I wasn't aware that you received any," sneered the squire.

"I have just made an engagement to work for five dollars a week," said our hero, enjoying the squire's look of surprise.

"Indeed! Who pays you that?"

"A gentleman boarding at the hotel has engaged me to read to him as his eyes are weak."

"A fool and his money are soon parted," said Squire Leech. "You may retain the position a week."

"I hope to keep it. I feel sure that I shall."

"I don't," said the squire, emphatically.

"Then are you willing to wait—say two weeks—for the rest of the interest?"

"No, I am not, and you ought to have known I

shouldn't be. There is a way of arranging the whole matter."

"By selling the place, you mean?"

"Yes; I mean just that. It is folly for you to think of keeping the property with such a heavy mortgage upon it on which you are unable to pay the interest. I have offered you a fair price for it."

"You offered four hundred dollars less than it cost."

"That is nonsense! It never cost fifteen hundred dollars."

"I have my husband's word for it," said the widow.

"Then, he made some mistake, you may be sure."

"I am sure father was right," said Herbert. "Besides, we have his bills to prove it."

"That's neither here nor there," said Squire Leech, impatiently. "Even if it cost ten thousand dollars, it's only worth eleven hundred now; that is to say, three hundred and fifty dollars over and above the mortgage."

"You are hard upon me, Squire Leech," said Mrs. Carter, despondently.

"You are a woman, ma'am, and women never understand business. I make allowance for you; but your son ought to know better than to encourage you."

"I want my mother to be treated fairly and justly."

"Do you mean to imply that I would treat her otherwise, young man?" demanded the squire, angrily. "I advise you not to make an enemy of me."

Herbert looked sober. The squire might not be right but certainly he had the power to carry his point and that power he was certain to exercise.

"Will you give my mother and myself a little time to consult what is to be done?" he asked.

"Yes," said the squire, feeling that he had carried his point. "I might refuse, of course, but I wish to be easy with you and therefore I will give you till half past twelve. I will be back at that time."

He took his cane and left the house.

His reference to the post office reminded Herbert of the letter he had in his pocket for his mother.

"Here's a letter for you, mother," he said.

"A letter! Who can it be from?"

"It's postmarked at Randolph," said Herbert.

"Perhaps it's from Aunt Nancy," suggested the widow. "I don't know anyone else in Randolph that would be likely to write to me."

She opened the envelope and uttered a cry of surprise as two bills dropped out and fluttered to the floor.

Herbert picked them up eagerly and cried: "Why, mother, they are ten-dollar bills. Twenty dollars in all!"

"Twenty dollars!" repeated Mrs. Carter, in amazement.

"Hurrah! now we can pay the interest!" exclaimed Herbert. "Won't the squire be mad!" and he laughed joyously. "Read the letter aloud, mother."

Mrs. Carter read as follows:

"MY DEAR NIECE: I have thought of you often, and wish we were not so far distant from each other. I should enjoy seeing you and that good son of yours often. I am afraid you have had a hard time getting along. My wants are few and I have more than enough to supply them. I inclose twenty dollars in this letter. I shall not need them, for an old woman like me can live on very little.

"I wish you would write to me sometimes or ask Herbert to. I feel lonely and it would be a great favor to me. If it were not so far, I would ask you and Herbert to come over and spend a day or two with me. Perhaps you can manage to do it some time. Only don't delay too long, for I am getting old and can't expect to live much longer.
"Your affectionate aunt,
"NANCY CARTER."

"How good of Aunt Nancy! If her brother had possessed her kind heart, we should be better off to-day."

"It came just in the nick of time, mother. How lucky!"

"Say, rather, how providential, my son. We owe this to the kindness of God. He will not see us want."

"Of course you are right, mother; but the squire won't regard it in the same light. He will be terribly disappointed, for he thinks he has got us in his power."

"I am thankful that this is to be our home for six months more."

"Longer than that, mother. I am earning something now, and I will save up money to pay our next interest."

"Squire Leech is coming back," said Mrs. Carter.

"See how briskly he walks!" said Herbert. "I don't think he'll be so cheerful when he leaves the house."

"I don't think we ought to exult, Herbert."

"I can't help it, mother and I'm not ashamed of it, either. You are carrying benevolence too far."

Here the squire's knock was heard, and Herbert went to admit him.

CHAPTER XVIII

HOW THE SQUIRE WAS CIRCUMVENTED

THE squire was in very good spirits. All the way back from the post office he had been congratulating himself on the elegant bargain he was about to make. The widow and her son had been obliged to yield. Squire Leech thought more of Herbert than of his mother, for he was convinced that but for him he could have talked over Mrs. Carter six months before.

"Serves the boy right," he said to himself. "It was preposterous in him to oppose my wishes. He might have known I would advise what was best."

The squire meant what was best for him. He had not given much thought what would be best for Mrs. Carter.

"Some men would take advantage of their situation and reduce their offer," thought the squire, virtuously, "but I won't be hard on them. They shall have the three hundred and fifty dollars."

"Well," said he cheerfully, as Herbert opened the door, "I believe I have given you the time I agreed upon."

"Yes, sir," said Herbert. "Please walk in."

The squire expected to find him sober and depressed, but in spite of himself Herbert could not help looking in good spirits. This puzzled the squire a little, but he said to himself: "Probably they have decided that my offer wasn't so bad a one, after all."

"Well," said the village magnate, "well, Mrs. Carter, now that you have had time to think over my proposal, you have probably seen its advantages."

"I should not be willing to give up the house, sir. My husband built it, and——"

The squire's brow darkened. What a perverse, obstinate woman she was!

"That ain't the question," he exclaimed, pounding his cane on the floor. "There are many things we don't want to do that we've got to do. You stand in your own light, ma'am. I have my rights."

"We don't deny that, sir," said Herbert, who enjoyed the squire's excitement, knowing how it must end.

"I am glad to hear it," said the squire; "but it appears to me you think you and your mother are the only persons to be considered in this matter."

"I think my mother is entitled to some consideration."

"Haven't I considered her? Haven't I offered her a most liberal price for the place?"

"We don't call it liberal."

"Then you are unreasonable. Many men in my position would offer less. Indeed, I don't think I ought to offer more than three hundred dollars."

"We would thank you, Squire Leech, if we could see

any favor in offering three or four hundred dollars less than the house is worth."

"We have had enough of this nonsense," said the squire, angrily. "It is not too late to withdraw my offer."

"You had better withdraw it," said Herbert, composedly, "for mother and I have decided to refuse it."

"Refuse it!" gasped the squire. "What do you mean by such outrageous impudence?"

"I don't see how it can be considered impudence. We are not obliged to accept every offer made us."

"You are obliged to accept this," cried Squire Leech, stamping his cane upon the floor again. "You know there is no help for it."

"How do you make that out, sir?" inquired our hero.

"You can't pay the interest."

"I beg your pardon, sir; we are ready to pay."

"I mean the whole of the interest."

"So do I."

"It must be paid at once."

"It shall be paid at once, Squire Leech. Please make out a receipt."

Squire Leech was never more astonished in his life. He was not convinced till Herbert produced what he could distinguish as two ten-dollar bills and one five.

"There will be two dollars and a half change," said Herbert in a business-like manner.

"What did you mean by telling me you could not pay the interest when I was here at twelve o'clock?"

"We could not, then, or thought we could not."

"Then how can you pay me now?"

"We received some money in a letter this morning. The letter had not been opened when you were here, so we didn't know we could meet your claims."

Squire Leech was very angry. He felt that he had been defeated, and that triumph had slipped over to the other side. But he resolved to make one more attempt.

"I have the right to refuse this money," he said. "It comes too late. It should have been paid at twelve."

"I beg your pardon, Squire Leech; you yourself gave us time to consult what to do."

"Because," said the squire, unguardedly, "I thought you could not pay the interest."

Herbert could not help smiling.

"We have nothing to do with what you thought."

The squire frowned and bit his lips with vexation. He tried to think of some way of getting over the difficulty but none presented itself. As he dashed off the signature and took the money, he said, angrily: "The time will come when I will have this place. Your convenient letters won't always come just in the nick of time."

"I hope to be prepared for you next time, without having to depend on that."

Still, the squire lingered. The fact was, that, though very angry, he was anxious to know from whom Mrs. Carter had received this opportune help.

"Who sent you this letter?" he asked.

"I don't think we need to tell you that," said Herbert.

"I have no objection to tell," said Mrs. Carter. "It was my aunt, Nancy Carter, of Randolph, who so kindly remembered us."

"I wish she'd kept back her letter a day or two," thought the squire.

"Is she rich?" he asked, abruptly.

"No; she has a very modest income left by her brother; but her wants are few, and she thought we might need help. She has a good heart."

"Well, ma'am, as my business is over, I will leave you," said the squire, sulkily. "As for that boy of yours," pointing his finger at Herbert, "I advise you to teach him better manners. He won't gain anything by his impertinence. If he had acted differently I would have given him employment, or got my superintendent to do so."

"I should have been unable to accept it, Squire Leech," said Herbert. "I have made an engagement already."

The squire had forgotten this, and it was mortifying to expect that his patronage was of no importance to the boy whom he detested.

"Good morning!" he said abruptly and left the room.

"I am afraid, Herbert, you treated the squire disrespectfully," said Mrs. Carter.

"I don't think so, mother, unless to oppose his wishes is to be disrespectful."

"He spoke as if he thought you did."

"I know that, but he wouldn't if he hadn't been unreasonable. But I've got to go to the hotel in fifteen minutes. Just give me a bite, for I'm awful hungry."

So the day which Herbert had so much dreaded in advance was marked by two pieces of good luck.

CHAPTER XIX

HERBERT BECOMES A PROFESSOR

WHEN Herbert reached the hotel he went up at once to Mr. Cameron's room.

"I believe I am a little late," he said, apologetically; "but I was detained at home by a matter of business."

"You are young to have your time occupied by matters of business," said the young man, smiling.

"Yes, if my father were alive it would not devolve upon me, but my mother generally consults with me."

"I hope your business was arranged satisfactorily."

"Yes, but it came near turning out otherwise. I would like to tell you about it."

"Do so," said Mr. Cameron, kindly. "I shall be interested in whatever affects you."

Herbert gave an account of Squire Leech's attempts to get possession of their cottage.

"But for that letter of Aunt Nancy's," he concluded, "we should have been obliged to part with our house."

"For the paltry sum of twenty-two dollars and a half?"

"It wasn't paltry to us."

"No, to be sure. Why didn't you tell me this morning? I would have lent you the money."

"You would?" exclaimed Herbert.

"With pleasure."

"Thank you, Mr. Cameron," said our hero; "but I shouldn't have dared to ask such a favor of a stranger."

"I must tell you that this Squire Leech has probably taken advantage of your ignorance of business. I don't know exactly how the law is in this State, but I presume that, so far from the squire being authorized to take immediate possession of your place, he would be obliged to give legal notice of sale, on foreclosure of mortgage, by advertisement in some weekly paper. This would allow of sale at auction to the highest bidder."

"I didn't know that; I supposed the squire could order us out immediately and take possession."

"Squire Leech certainly knew better than that, but he evidently wanted to frighten your mother into selling to him at a sacrifice."

"That was mean," said Herbert, indignantly, "and he a rich man, too."

"I quite agree with you," said Mr. Cameron. "If you have any further difficulty with this grasping capitalist, come to me and I will give you the best advice I can."

"I will, Mr. Cameron, and thank you for your advice. You have relieved my mind. I will tell mother what you say. What would you like to have me read first?"

"We will put off the reading for a short time. I want to ask you a few more questions about yourself, not out of curiosity, but because I may, if I understand your circumstances, some time have it in my power to serve you."

"Thank you, sir. I shall be very glad to tell you anything. I was afraid you would not feel interested."

"You are my private secretary now and that insures my interest. How long since did your father die?"

"A little over a year."

"What was his business?"

"When he was a young man he was employed in a manufactory near Providence, but the confinement injured his health and he learned the carpenter's trade."

"I shouldn't think there would be much for a carpenter to do in a small village like this."

"My father managed to make a comfortable living but that was all. At the time he died, he considered that our house was mortgaged for only half its value, but Squire Leech thinks otherwise."

"Squire Leech wants to get possession of your place. So that was all your father was able to leave you?"

"No, not quite all; there was something else which father seemed to think was worth something, but I am afraid it will never do us any good."

"What is that?" asked Mr. Cameron.

"He was at work in his leisure for the last two years of his life on an invention."

"An invention! Of what nature?"

"You know I told you he was employed in a cotton manufactory when a young man. This made him familiar with spinning and weaving. He thought he could make an improvement in some of the machinery used and he worked out his idea in a wooden model."

"Have you the model?" asked Cameron, with interest.

"Yes, sir, and also a written paper describing the invention. A few days before he died father called me to his bedside and told me that he wanted me some day to show his invention to a manufacturer and get his opinion of it. He said that he hoped some time it would be a source of profit to mother and myself."

"Have you ever done as he advised?" asked Cameron.

"I have never had opportunity. There is no manufacturing town near here and I cannot afford to travel."

"I am myself the son of a cotton manufacturer," said Cameron, "and, though I have never been employed in the business, I have from my boyhood been accustomed to visit my father's factory. My opinion may be worth something, therefore. If you are willing to show me your father's model——"

"I shall be very much obliged to you if you will look at it," said Herbert. "I have been afraid that father exaggerated its value and that it might have defects which would prevent its being adopted anywhere."

"I will give you my opinion when I have seen it. And now suppose we set to work. Here is a treatise on logic. You may begin and read it very slowly, pausing at the end of every paragraph till I tell you to go on."

Herbert began to read as he had been requested. For the first two or three times he took very little interest in his subject and thought it very dry. In fact, it was not till he began to re-read the earlier portions that he could comprehend much of it.

"Now," said Cameron, after he had read half an hour, "I have something else for you to do. You are not only my reader, but I must make you my teacher, too."

Herbert laughed, saying: "I think you'll have to get somebody that knows more than I, then; I wouldn't venture to teach a college student."

"I mean that you shall hear my lessons. I want you to imagine yourself a college professor and ask me questions on what you have just read."

"Do you think I can?"

"You may bungle a little at first, but you'll improve. If you do well, when I get through with you I will try to get you a professor's chair at some college."

"I should like that, if professors get well paid."

"They generally get more than five dollars a week; but that is all that I can afford to pay at present."

"I'm only an apprentice," said Herbert smiling, "and am quite satisfied."

Herbert began to question Cameron on what he had been reading. He did not find it altogether easy, partly from want of practice, partly because the subject was one he knew nothing about. But whenever blunders were made Cameron laughed good-naturedly and the young professor joined in the merriment.

"We'll take political economy next," said the student. "You won't find that so dry as logic."

Though political economy is generally studied in the junior or senior year at college, its principles, if familiarly illustrated, are not beyond the comprehension of a boy of fifteen. He found himself reading with interest, and when he came to act the rôle of professor he acquitted himself more creditably than with logic.

"I think," said Cameron, "I shall recommend you for the chair of political economy."

"I like it much better," said Herbert.

"So do I. Still, logic is important in its way. To-morrow I must try you on Latin."

"I am afraid it won't be much use," said our hero. "I have studied it a little two winters when we had a college student keeping our winter school."

"If you know as much as that you will answer my purpose better than I anticipated. Now we'll take a walk. You shall show me the houses of Wrayburn."

"The houses of Wrayburn are four in number," said Herbert; "the two churches, the town hall, and Squire Leech's house."

"There's another walk which I prefer; I mean to Prospect Pond. Suppose we walk over to it."

"I shall be glad to," said Herbert.

"You are a very accommodating professor. You let me off from study when I feel lazy."

CHAPTER XX

PROSPECT POND

It was a beautiful afternoon and Herbert was satisfied to lay books aside and walk over to Prospect Pond.

This pond was about a mile from the village and probably about a mile and a half in circuit. At the farther end was a small hill crowned with forest trees.

"That would be a fine situation for a house."

"Yes," said Herbert, "but it would be hard to get at."

"Oh, of course a road would have to be built connecting with the highway. Perhaps you will build a house there when you are a rich man."

"Then I shall have to wait a few years," said Herbert.

"You wouldn't be the first poor boy that has grown rich. My own father is rich now, but when he was of your age he was only a poor 'bobbin boy,' working at scanty pay in the factory of which he is now owner."

"I should like to be rich for my mother's sake," said Herbert.

"With money one can do a great deal of good, though not all rich men choose to apply their riches worthily. How smooth the water is to-day! Isn't there a boat somewhere that we can use?"

"There's one a few rods from here, but it belongs to James Leech."

"Would it do to take it, do you think?"

"It might do for you but not for me."

"Why not for you?"

"James and I are not very good friends."

"Why not?"

"He looks down upon me because I am poor."

Prospect Pond

"So he is inclined to put on airs on account of his father's money?"

"I should say he is."

"Let us go and see the boat at any rate."

Herbert led the way through a meadow to a clump of trees, where a small rowboat floated upon the water.

"Does Leech often go out in it?"

"Two or three times a week."

"It is just about large enough for two, though it would easily accommodate one more."

"Yes."

"If I thought your friend would not be round I should be tempted to try it for half an hour."

"I think you might venture."

"Jump in, then, and we'll push out."

Herbert shook his head.

"If the boat belonged to anyone but James Leech I would go; but I don't like him well enough to take any liberty with anything of his."

"Perhaps you are right. Would you mind sitting down and waiting for me twenty minutes or half an hour?"

"Oh, no; it will be pleasant."

"Then here goes."

Cameron jumped into the boat, pushed off and began to row in a style that showed he was accustomed to the exercise. The pond was so small that it was not easy for him to get out of sight.

Herbert sat down, not without a secret longing to be in the boat also; but he did not care to place himself under any obligations to James.

Suddenly he heard a hasty step behind him. Looking up, he saw the owner of the boat close at hand.

James Leech looked for his boat and saw that it was gone. Then his gaze fell upon our hero.

"What have you done with my boat, Carter?" he demanded, peremptorily.

"What makes you ask such a question, Leech?" answered Herbert.

"Why do you call me Leech?" said James, angrily.

"For the same reason you call me Carter, I suppose."

"There's a great difference between us," said James.

"That's true," assented Herbert.

"And you ought to treat me with proper respect."

"I treat you with all the respect you deserve."

"You haven't answered my question," said James.

"What question?"

"Where is my boat?"

"Out on the pond. Look and you will see it."

James looked where Herbert pointed.

"Who is that in that boat?" he demanded, angrily.

"Mr. Cameron."

"Who's he?"

"A boarder at the hotel."

"Is it the young man from Yale College? My father was speaking of him this morning," said James, moderating his tone very considerably.

"Yes."

"Then I don't mind. My father says he is very rich. I suppose I shall be introduced to him soon," said James, complacently.

"If you will wait a few minutes till he comes ashore I will introduce you," said Herbert.

"You! What do you know of him?" sneered James.

"I passed the afternoon with him," said Herbert.

"He must be hard up for company," said James.

"Look here, James Leech," said Herbert his eyes flashing; "I've had enough of that kind of talk. I don't intend to submit to your impudence. When you speak to me keep a civil tongue in your head."

"I never heard such impudence. What do you mean by addressing me in that style?"

"What do I mean? I mean to warn you to be civil."

"Look here, Carter! I'll tell my father and he'll turn you out of house and home," exclaimed James, furiously.

"He hasn't the power, fortunately."

"Hasn't he got a mortgage on your place?"

"Yes; but the interest was paid to-day and no more will be due for six months."

"Where did you get the money to pay the interest?"

"That is no business of yours. It is enough for you to know that it is paid and that your father has no more control over us than we have over him."

James was disappointed. He had expected that the interest would not be paid and that Mrs. Carter and Herbert would be at his father's mercy. It was certainly surprising that they had raised the money.

"Are you waiting here for Mr. Cameron?" asked James.

"Yes."

"I don't think you need to."

"As you don't even know him, I don't think your opinions as to his wishes of much importance."

"I wouldn't thrust myself on him, if I were you."

"Thank you, I don't intend to."

"I suppose you fell in with him by accident. He probably don't know who you are."

"Oh, yes, he does. He knows all about me. I am going to spend to-morrow afternoon with him also," said Herbert, delighting to mystify his companion.

"He won't care to have you call much longer. My aunt has written to my father about him and he will invite Mr. Cameron to call."

"I have no objection but I don't think it will make any difference as I am Mr. Cameron's private secretary."

"Private secretary! What do you do?"

"I read to him, as his eyes are poor, and I suppose I shall write for him when he needs it."

"What does he pay you?"

"I don't know as that concerns you particularly. Still, I don't mind telling you. He pays me five dollars a week."

"That's a good deal more than you're worth."

"I think so myself, especially as I only spend the afternoon with him."

James was quite annoyed to find that the boy he disliked was prospering so well. He was about to make another unpleasant remark when Herbert suddenly exclaimed:

"He's turned the boat. Doesn't he row beautifully?"

The same thought sprang up in the minds of both boys: "I wish I could row like that."

CHAPTER XXI

ROWING

The little boat touched its moorings.

"Mr. Cameron," said Herbert, "allow me to introduce to you the owner of the boat, Mr. James Leech."

"Mr. Leech," said Cameron, "I have to apologize for taking your boat without leave. I hope I haven't kept you waiting for it."

If the young collegian had not been the son of a wealthy man, whose social position was higher than his own, James would not so readily have accepted the apology. As it was, he said, graciously: "Oh it's no matter. I'm glad you took the boat. How beautifully you row!"

"Thank you for the compliment. Last year I belonged to the Sophomore crew at Yale."

"I wish I could row as well as you."

"It is a matter of practice. If I can give you any hints I shall be glad to do so."

"Thank you," said James, eagerly. "Would you have time this afternoon?"

"Yes, I have an hour to spare. If you and my friend Herbert will get into the boat and row out a little way, I shall get an idea of your style of rowing."

"I would rather row out alone," said James, haughtily, with a disparaging look at Herbert.

"Unfortunately that won't do as well. You must learn to row with one oar first."

"Then suppose you get into the boat with me."

"That won't do as well. I am much heavier than you. Now you and Herbert are about the same weight."

"Very well, then," said James, and turning to Herbert, he said, ungraciously: "Will you row with me?"

"If you desire it," said Herbert.

"Get in, then."

When they returned Cameron made some criticisms upon their rowing. They started out again but Herbert profited better by the instructions he had received and the young collegian said so when they returned.

James was far from liking this and when Cameron asked him if he would try another row he answered: "No, I am tired of it."

"If you get tired so soon, I am afraid you will have to strengthen your arms by gymnastic exercises."

"Oh, I am not tired. I don't feel like rowing."

"Then suppose we walk back to the village. Does your way lie with ours?"

"Nearly all the way," said James.

He enjoyed the idea of walking with the collegian, but it was rather a drawback that Herbert was to share that pleasure with him. Still he could not very well suggest that Herbert should leave them.

"Have you seen my father's house?" asked James.

"Perhaps, without knowing whose it was."

"You couldn't help knowing it. It is the best in the village," said James, pompously.

Cameron looked at him curiously.

"If he comes to Yale," he thought, "and puts on these airs, he'll be taken down without ceremony."

"Oh, indeed!" he said aloud, dryly.

"Are you going to stay here long?" asked James.

"I can't say how long. I am here for my health."

"You must come and see us. My father will be very glad to see you. My aunt has written us about you."

"Indeed! May I ask your aunt's name?"

"Her name is Davenport—Mrs. John Davenport. She lives in New Haven."

"Oh, yes, I have met her."

Cameron smiled to himself. The lady referred to was not unlike her brother and nephew, being pompous and presuming—one, indeed, whom he secretly disliked.

"She wants me to prepare for Yale," said James.

"Of course we Yale men are biased, but we think no student can do better than to come to Yale."

"My father wants me to be a professional man—a lawyer."

"A good profession. Do you think you should like it?"

"Yes," said James, complacently. "It's a very genteel profession. Besides, most of our public men are lawyers. I might stand a chance to get into public life."

"Should you like it?"

"Yes, I should like to be a member of Congress. My father has a good deal of influence and I am his only son, so I should have a very good chance; don't you think so?"

"It would seem so," said Cameron, with a quiet smile. "I think you had better come to Yale. You would be improved in many ways."

He referred to the possibility of James having some of the self-conceit taken out of him; but then the squire's son interpreted the remark as a compliment.

"Have you ever thought of going to college, Herbert?" asked Cameron, turning to our hero.

"I always thought I should like to go," answered Herbert, "but I never thought there was any chance of it."

James laughed scornfully.

"No, I should think not," he said.

"Why?" asked Cameron, meaning to draw him out.

"He's too poor," said James.

"You, I suppose, have no trouble in that way?"

"My father is the richest man in Wrayburn."

"That is lucky for you," said the collegian.

"I shouldn't like to be as poor as Carter."

"It isn't pleasant or convenient to be poor," said Herbert, quietly. "I don't mean always to be poor."

"You probably will be," said James.

"Poor boys don't always stay poor."

"There isn't much chance for you to rise."

"I don't know why," said Herbert.

"Then it seems, Herbert," said Cameron, smiling, "there is not much chance of my welcoming you at Yale."

"I wish there was."

"So you will have to be content with serving as my professor here."

James did not understand this allusion, but privately wondered how Cameron could talk so intimately with a boy in Herbert's low social position.

"I turn off here," he said. "That is our house."

"Is it?" said Cameron, indifferently.

"Your friend seems to have a very vain idea of his high position," said Cameron, when James was out of hearing.

"And a very low idea of mine," added Herbert.

"Does that disturb you?"

"A little. He carries it so far as to be annoying."

"Circumstances may change with you both."

"I hope they may with me," said Herbert. "I don't want James to come down in the world, but I hope to rise."

The next day Cameron was honored by a special call from Squire Leech, who left an invitation for the young collegian to take tea with him the following afternoon. This invitation Cameron accepted.

CHAPTER XXII

ANDREW TEMPLE

ABOUT half-past four o'clock one afternoon a tall, dark-complexioned man, wearing a white hat, inscribed his name in the register of the Wrayburn hotel.

"Can you tell where Mr. Leech lives?" he inquired of the landlord.

"He lives about a quarter of a mile from here. I can send some one with you to show you the house."

Just then Herbert came downstairs from Mr. Cameron.

"Herbert," said the landlord, "here is a gentleman wants to go to Squire Leech's. Would you mind showing him the way?"

"I will do so with pleasure," said our hero, politely. "Are you ready to go now, sir?"

"Yes," said the stranger. "Landlord, please assign me a room and have my bag carried up."

"All right, sir."

"Now, my lad, I am ready. It isn't far, is it?"

"About five minutes' walk—that is all, sir."

"I never was in Wrayburn—much going on here?"

"Not much, sir. It is a quiet town."

"Mr. Leech—Squire Leech, I think you call him—was an old schoolmate of mine. We went to the Brandon Academy together. I suppose he is rich, eh?"

"He is the richest man in Wrayburn."

"I am glad to hear it," said the other, in a tone of satisfaction. "What do you think he is worth?"

Andrew Temple 101

"Some say a hundred thousand dollars."

"Very good!" commented Andrew Temple, for this was his name in the hotel register—"for the country, I mean. In the city that wouldn't make a rich man."

"Wouldn't it?" asked Herbert, who had supposed a man worth a hundred thousand dollars rich anywhere.

"No, to be sure not. It costs a great deal more to live. Why, I myself am worth something like that; but in New York nobody regards me as rich."

"I should feel rich with ten thousand," said Herbert.

"That would about pay my expenses for a year."

"Squire Leech doesn't spend anywhere near that. I don't believe it costs him two thousand dollars a year."

"Very likely. There's a great deal of difference between the country and the city."

"Is it easy to make money in the city?" asked Herbert.

"Yes, if a man is sharp and has some money to start with. Do you think of going there?"

"I am afraid it would be of no use. I have no money to start with, and I am afraid I am not smart."

"Wait and I may give you a lift. Here's my card."

"Thank you, sir," said Herbert, as he read: "Andrew Temple, No. — Nassau Street, Room 12."

"That's my office; I speculate in stocks."

"Is that a good business?"

"Capital, if you know the ropes. If you ever come to the city, call at my office."

"Thank you, sir. Here is Squire Leech's house."

"I am much obliged to you. Allow me to compensate you for your trouble"; and Mr. Temple thrust his thumb and forefinger into his vest pocket.

"Oh, no, sir, I don't want pay," said Herbert, hurriedly.

Mr. Temple had made the offer as a matter of form and was relieved to find it declined. He said "good-night" graciously and advanced to the front door.

"Is Squire Leech at home?" he inquired of the servant.

"Yes, sir; I believe so. Won't you walk in?"

"Thank you. Please hand your master that card."

Squire Leech did not recall Mr. Temple's name, and greeted him distantly. Not so Mr. Temple. He rose, and shook the squire's passive hand energetically.

"Why, Leech, it seems like old times seeing you again."

"You have the advantage of me," said the squire.

"You don't mean to say you've forgotten Temple—Andrew Temple? Why, we were at the Brandon Academy together."

"I suppose I ought to remember you."

"To be sure you ought. We were very good friends in the old days."

One reason of the squire's distant manner was that Mr. Temple, though a rich man according to his own account, had a somewhat seedy look. The squire was afraid he intended to ask for help on the score of old friendship. It was with a hesitating voice, therefore, that he asked:

"How has the world treated you?"

"I am not rich, to be sure. Probably I am not worth more than a hundred thousand dollars, at the outside; but before five years roll over my head, I see my way clear to half a million.

Squire Leech's manner changed instantaneously.

"I am glad to see you," he said, cordially. "How long have you been in town?"

"Only just arrived. I inquired my way here as soon as I heard that you were living here."

"Are you at the hotel?"

"Yes. I left my luggage there."

"You must come and stop with me. We will talk over old times."

"Thank you; it would be much pleasanter for me, of course. In fact, I came to Wrayburn on account of your being here. I happened to be in the neighborhood, and I said 'I must see Leech at any rate.' So here I am. Fortune has smiled on you, I hope?"

"Yes," said the squire, "I am comfortable."

"The boy that guided me here said that you were the richest man in Wrayburn."

"I believe I am," said the squire, complacently. "I am worth somewhere about the same as you."

"That's fair; it is more for you than for me. It costs me ten thousand dollars a year to live in the city."

"Does it?" inquired Leech.

"I've sometimes thought of going to the country, where my expenses would be much less; but, after all, you can make much more money in the city."

"You think there are opportunities of making money rapidly there?" asked his companion.

"No doubt of it."

"I should like to talk with you on that subject after supper. Now, I will go and tell Mrs. Leech you are here. We will send for your carpetbag after supper."

Squire Leech was a covetous man. He had a passion for money-making and he had availed himself of all the opportunities which the country afforded. He had about as much property as his friend. He began to think he had been plodding along in a very slow, unsatisfactory manner. He would make careful inquiries and perhaps Temple would put him in the way of doubling his money. Upon the whole, therefore, he was very glad to see Mr. Temple, and introduced him to his wife and son as an old schoolmate with whom he had once been very intimate.

CHAPTER XXIII

TEMPLE THE TEMPTER

"THIS is my son, James, Mr. Temple," said the squire, as that young gentleman came in to supper a little late.

"Indeed! How old are you, James?"

James took in at a glance the visitor's appearance, which did not give the impression of prosperity, and answered, with haughty condescension: "I am almost sixteen."

"I congratulate you, Mr. Leech," said Temple. "I am not blessed with a son. I would gladly give twenty thousand dollars could I have a son of your boy's age."

James pricked up his ears. Temple spoke as if he had the twenty thousand dollars to give. He must be a man of property and so entitled to respect.

"What are you going to do with your boy?"

"I have not decided. Perhaps he may go to college."

"I think I shall be a lawyer," said James.

"A good profession. Some of our New York lawyers make great incomes."

"Do you live in New York?" asked James.

"Yes; that is my residence. You must establish yourself in the city when you are ready to practice."

"That is just what I want to do; I don't want to bury myself in a one-horse country town like this."

"And be a one-horse lawyer," suggested Temple, laughing. "Quite right, my young friend. In the city alone you will find a broad field of action."

"That's just the way I think," said James.

"I needn't say I would do all in my power to push you, and I flatter myself I have some influence."

"You are very kind, Mr. Temple," said Mrs. Leech; "but I hoped that James could still continue to live with us."

"You can't expect me to live at home all my life," said James, impatiently.

"Perhaps your husband may be persuaded himself to remove to the city," said Temple. "I really think he stands in his own light in staying in a small place like this."

"Just so," said James, who would have liked nothing

better than to live in New York. "There is no society here. I have no boys to associate with in my own position. Why won't you move to New York, father?"

"That requires consideration," said Squire Leech.

"I should like to talk with you on that subject after supper," said Temple. "Mrs. Leech, may I ask for another cup of tea?"

When supper was over Squire Leech led the way into the sitting room, and his guest followed. The vista of future wealth which his visitor had opened to him had not been without its effect and he began to make inquiries.

"I suppose," he said, "there are ways of investing money to good advantage in New York?"

"Most certainly—many ways."

"Real estate?"

"That may do, but it is too slow for me. I owned a house uptown. I sold for thirty thousand dollars. In six weeks I made twenty thousand more out of it."

"Is it possible?" ejaculated the squire. "Twenty thousand, did you say?"

"To be sure. Of course that was extra good luck. You can't expect to do as well often, but there are always ways of turning over capital."

"May I ask in what way you made this large sum?"

"To be sure. I speculated in Erie. It is all the time fluctuating. I became convinced that it was on the rise. I went in and the event justified my action."

Temple spoke quietly, as if it were no great matter, after all. His host was very much impressed, and felt like a man who has discovered a gold mine. He had succeeded in saving up about two thousand dollars a year for some years; but what was that to twenty thousand dollars made in six weeks? Still, prudence led him to suggest: "But isn't there danger of losing heavily?"

"Not if you are acquainted with the stock market. It is the ignoramuses that get bit."

"I know very little of the stock market myself," confessed Squire Leech. "I own some bank stocks."

"No money to be made in bank stocks."

"They pay good dividends."

"No doubt; but there is little or no variation in value. It's fluctuation that gives a man a chance."

"I should be as likely to lose as gain, knowing as little as I do of the market."

"True; but I should be happy to place my knowledge at your disposal. As an old friend and schoolmate I naturally feel interested in your prosperity."

"You are very kind," said the squire; "but wouldn't it be too much trouble?"

"Not at all. In fact, it's my business, and wouldn't inconvenience me in the least. By the way, how is your property invested?" asked Temple, carelessly.

"Mostly in real estate."

"It must pay you very little."

"That is true. After deducting taxes and repairs, there is very little left."

"So I supposed. It would pay you to mortgage your property, or sell it, and use the money in Wall Street."

"I have about twenty thousand dollars in bank stock."

"That could readily be sold."

"What investments would you suggest?"

"I couldn't tell you on the moment; but I think favorably of a mining stock lately put on the market. I have private advices that it is likely to develop extraordinary richness, and the stock may even treble in three months."

"Where is the mine?" asked the squire, eagerly.

"Out in Nevada. A friend of mine has just returned from there and he has given me strictly confidential information in regard to it. He has so much faith in it that he has bought fifteen thousand dollars' worth of shares."

"Could I get any?" asked Squire Leech.

"I think you could if you go to work quietly. If you went into the market openly, they would suspect something and raise the price on you."

"Yes, I see. Do you think that is better than Erie?"

"At present, nothing is to be made in Erie. It is likely to go down before it goes up. The time may come when you can buy to advantage but not now."

"I have a great mind to go up to the city with you, and investigate the matter," said the squire.

"Do so, by all means. I shall be delighted, and will cheerfully render you all the assistance in my power. But, my friend, let me give you one piece of advice."

"What is that?"

"Say as little as possible to your wife on the subject. Women don't understand business. They are frightened at risks and don't understand speculation."

"I think you are correct," said his host. "Men must judge for themselves. It is a weak man who would be guided by his wife."

"So I say. Why, my wife happened to learn that I had gone into Erie on the occasion I mentioned. She remonstrated in great alarm; but when I announced that I had cleared twenty thousand dollars, she had no more to say."

The next day they went to New York together and within a week the squire had bought largely in the Nevada mine. He subscribed to a financial paper, and was fully embarked on the dangerous sea of speculation.

CHAPTER XXIV

JAMES IS SNUBBED

In accordance with the invitation, Cameron walked over to supper with Squire Leech. His social position as the son of a rich manufacturer insured him a cordial welcome and great attention from the whole family.

"You must find our village very dull, Mr. Cameron," said his host.

"Oh, no, sir; I think I shall enjoy it very well."

"We have very little good society, I am sorry to say."

"That's so, father," broke in James. "I wish you would move to the city."

"That may come some day," said his father, thinking of Mr. Temple and his operations.

"How do you occupy your time, Mr. Cameron?" asked Mrs. Leech.

"I walk about in the forenoon. In the afternoon I am occupied with my professor," answered the young man.

"Your professor!" repeated the lady, in surprise. "Is one of your college professors staying here?"

"No; they are too busy to leave New Haven. I refer to my young reader, Herbert Carter."

"Herbert Carter!" repeated James, scornfully.

"Yes," said Cameron, ignoring the scorn; "he reads my lessons to me and then questions me upon them. That is why I call him my professor."

"I should hardly think you would find him competent," said the squire.

"He don't know much," said James, contemptuously.

"On the contrary, I find him very intelligent. He reads clearly and distinctly, and I congratulate myself on obtaining so satisfactory an assistant."

Squire Leech shrugged his shoulders and had too much wisdom to continue detracting from Herbert's merits, seeing that his guest seemed determined to think well of him. Not so James.

"He is from a low family," he said, spitefully.

"Low?" interrogated Cameron, significantly.

"His mother is very poor."

"That's a very different thing," observed Cameron.

"Mrs. Carter is a very respectable person," said the squire, condescendingly. "Indeed, I have offered to re-

James is Snubbed

lieve her by taking her house at a high valuation; but, under a mistaken idea of her own interest, she refuses to sell."

"But you'll get it finally, father," asked James.

"I shall probably have to take it in the end, as I have a mortgage on it for nearly its value."

Cameron looked down upon his plate and said nothing.

"My son will be happy to accompany you about the neighborhood, Mr. Cameron," said Squire Leech.

"I can go round with you 'most any time," said James.

"Thank you both. You are very kind," said Cameron, politely, but without expressing any pleasure.

"I think I may send James to Yale," observed his host. "I have a high idea of your college, Mr. Cameron."

"Thank you. I think your son could hardly fail of deriving benefit from a residence at Yale."

"James is my only child and I intend him to enjoy the greatest educational advantages. I should like to have him become a professional man."

"I should like to be a lawyer; that's a very gentlemanly profession," said James.

"You might rise to be a judge," said Cameron, with a smile.

"Very likely," said James, in a matter-of-course way, that amused the young man exceedingly.

"What an odious young cub!" he said to himself, as he wended his way back to the hotel at ten o'clock. "I never met such a combination of pride and self-conceit."

James thought Cameron had taken a fancy to him.

"He must get awfully tired of that low-bred Herbert Carter," he said to himself. "I guess I'll go round to-morrow morning and take a walk with him."

He met Cameron on the steps of the hotel.

"I thought I'd come and walk with you," he said.

"Very well," said Cameron. "Do you know the way to Mr. Crane's?"

"The carpenter's?"

"Yes."

"There's nothing to see there," said James.

"I beg your pardon. I want to see Herbert at his work."

"Oh, well, I'll show you the way," said James.

Herbert was hard at work when the two came up.

"How are you, professor?" asked Cameron.

"Very well, Mr. Cameron. How are you, James?"

"I'm well enough," answered James, who always found it hard to be decently civil to our hero. "Don't you get tired working?"

"I haven't worked long enough this morning for that. I dare say I shall be tired before noon."

"Then your other work will begin," said Cameron.

"That kind of work will be a rest to me, it's so different."

"If you had an extra hoe I would help you a little. It would be as good as exercise in the gymnasium."

"Perhaps I could borrow two and so employ both of you," remarked Herbert, with a glance at James, who was sprucely dressed and wore a flower in his buttonhole.

"None for me, thank you," said James, with a look of disgust. "I don't intend to become a laborer."

"You'll have to labor if you study law," said Cameron.

"That's genteel; besides I don't call it labor. Shall we go on, Mr. Cameron?"

"Not just yet. I want to watch Herbert a little longer."

So he lingered, much to the dissatisfaction of James.

"Won't you go out rowing?" he asked, when they were walking away.

"I have no objection," said Cameron; and they spent an hour on the pond.

"Do you think I can get into the crew if I go to Yale?" asked James, complacently.

James is Snubbed

"I should say not, unless you improve in rowing."

"Don't I row well?"

"There is considerable room for improvement. However, you have time enough for that."

They were cruising near the shore when a boy of ten came down to the bank and called out to them.

"James," he said, "will you let me go across in the boat with you?"

"Why should I?" demanded James, not very amicably, for the boy belonged to what he termed the lower classes.

"Do let me," urged the boy. "I left mother very sick and went for the doctor. She was all alone and I want to get back as soon as I can."

By the road the boy would have to walk about a mile and a quarter, while he could be rowed across the pond in six or seven minutes.

"I can't take anybody and everybody in my boat," said James, disagreeably. "Go ahead and walk."

"How can you refuse the boy, when he wants to get home to his sick mother?" said Cameron, indignantly. "Jump in, my boy, and we'll take you over."

"I don't know about that," said James, sullenly.

"Look here!" said Cameron, shortly. "Refuse this boy and I shall get out of the boat immediately and refuse hereafter to be seen in your company."

James was disagreeably surprised.

"Jump in, my boy," said Cameron, kindly.

"Thank you, sir," said the boy, gratefully. James was not a little mortified at the snubbing he had received, but he did not venture to expostulate.

Cameron was fond of boating, but did not care to be indebted to James for the loan of his boat.

"I'll have a boat sent on to me," he secretly determined, "and when I leave Wrayburn I'll give it to Herbert."

CHAPTER XXV

THE NEW BOAT

Herbert worked steadily every forenoon on his farm. Cameron then proposed that they should take the forenoon for their studies and walk out or exercise in some other way in the afternoon.

One afternoon Cameron said: "Let us take a walk to Prospect Pond; I think I should enjoy a little rowing."

"I will accompany you with pleasure, Mr. Cameron," said Herbert, "but don't ask me to go out in the boat with you."

"Why not? Are you afraid I will upset you?"

"No," answered Herbert; "I have confidence in your skill. Besides, I can swim."

"What is your objection, then?"

"If the boat belonged to anyone but James Leech I would not mind."

"Why should you mind that?"

"I met him last evening and he told me not to get into his boat again. He said he was perfectly willing you should use it, but he didn't choose to have me."

"It appears that I am a greater favorite with James Leech than you are," said Cameron, smiling.

"He looks down upon me as a poor boy."

"Well, I suppose James is entitled to his prejudice; but if you can't use the boat, I won't."

"Don't let that interfere with your pleasure, Mr. Cameron," said Herbert, eagerly. "I don't trouble myself in the least about the way James treats me."

"Let us go down to the pond, at any rate. We can sit down on the bank, if nothing better."

"All right."

An easy walk brought them to the edge of the pond.

The New Boat

Herbert naturally looked for James Leech's boat. He thought something was the matter with his eyes, for where there should be but one boat there were now two.

"Why, there's another boat!" he exclaimed.

"Is there?" asked Cameron, indifferently.

"Yes, don't you see it?"

"Well, it does look like a boat, I admit. I should say it was nicer than the other."

"I should say it was. Isn't she a regular beauty?" exclaimed Herbert, enthusiastically. "I wonder whose it is? James wouldn't want two."

There was a smile on Cameron's face that attracted Herbert's attention.

"Is it yours?" he asked.

"No; I know who owns it, though."

"It isn't the landlord, is it?"

"No."

"Then I can't imagine whose it is," said Herbert.

"Can't you?"

"No," said Herbert. "Will you tell me?"

"It is yours!"

"Mine!" exclaimed our hero, in the utmost surprise.

"Yes; I intended at first not to give it to you till I went away; but I may as well give it now, on one condition—that you let me use it whenever I please."

"How kind you are!" said Herbert, gratefully. "I never received such a splendid present in my life. I have done nothing to deserve it."

"Let me be the judge of that. Now, with your consent, we will try her."

With the utmost alacrity Herbert followed Cameron aboard the new craft, and took the oars. Smoothly and easily the boat glided off on the surface of the pond.

"I like it much better than James'," said Herbert.

"It's a better model. His is rather clumsy. Besides, this is new and he must have had his for some time."

"He has had it three years."

"It needs painting."

"Even if it were painted it wouldn't come up to this."

"I agree with you," said Cameron. "I am afraid James will be stirred with envy when he sees your boat."

"I am afraid so, too. He won't believe it is mine."

"It may be your duty, out of a delicate regard to his feelings, to give it up, or exchange," suggested Cameron.

"That's a little further than I carry my delicate regard to his feelings," responded Herbert.

After half an hour's rowing, Cameron said, suddenly: "I must go back to the hotel. I came near forgetting an important letter, which must be sent off by this afternoon's mail."

Herbert was a little disappointed, still he said, cheerfully: "All right, Mr. Cameron."

"Don't you cease your rowing," said the collegian.

"I thought you might not like to walk back alone."

"I don't mind that. I shall hurry back, and should be poor company. We will meet to-morrow morning."

Cameron set out on his return home. He had gone less than quarter of a mile when he met James Leech.

"Good afternoon, Mr. Cameron," said James, who was always polite to the rich manufacturer's son.

"Good afternoon, James."

"Won't you go out in my boat, Mr. Cameron?"

"Thank you, I have just returned from the pond. I am obliged to go back to the hotel to write a letter."

"I should have been glad of your company."

"You won't be alone," said Cameron, mischievously. "I left Herbert Carter at the pond."

"Was he out in the boat?" asked James, hastily.

"Yes."

Without a word James walked abruptly away. He was very angry with Herbert, who, he naturally concluded, was out in his boat.

"He's the most impudent and cheeky boy I ever met!" he said to himself. "Last evening, I positively forbade his getting into my boat and he don't take the slightest notice of it. He needn't think he can take such liberties."

Cameron smiled, as he read James' feelings in his face.

Just before reaching the pond there was rising ground, from which James could take a general survey of the lake. Herbert was cruising about and had not yet seen James.

"He don't think I'm so near," thought James. "He thinks I won't know anything about his impudence. I'll soon make him draw in his horns."

In his excitement, James did not notice the boat particularly. If he had he would have seen that it was not his boat. But, so far as he knew, there was no other boat on the pond. Indeed, there was no boy whose father could afford to buy him one, and James had come to think himself sole proprietor of the pond, as well as of the only craft that plied on its surface.

"I wonder," he thought, "whether I couldn't have Herbert fined for taking my property without leave, especially after I have expressly forbidden him to do it. I must ask my father this evening. It would bring down his pride a little to be taken before a justice."

Herbert had got tired of cruising, and made a vigorous stroke, as if to cross the pond. James put up his hand to his mouth and shouted at the top of his voice: "Come right back, Herbert Carter!"

CHAPTER XXVI

THE RIVAL BOATMEN

HERBERT, bending over his oars, heard the peremptory order of James to come back and smiled to himself as he instantly comprehended the mistake which the latter had made. From James' standpoint his own boat was not visible and it was not surprising that he should suspect our hero of having appropriated his boat.

"I won't undeceive him," he thought.

"What do you want?" he asked, resting on his oars, and looking back at James.

"You know what I want," said James, provoked.

"How should I know?"

"I want you to come right back, at once."

"What's happened? What am I wanted for?"

"You'll be wanted by the constable."

"I don't understand you," said Herbert, shrugging his shoulders. "You appear to be mad about something."

"So I am, and I have a right to be."

"Well, I'm sure I have no objection, if you like it."

James was pale with rage.

"Bring that boat right back here," he said.

"If you'll give me a good reason, perhaps I will; but I don't think it necessary to obey you without."

"You are a thief."

"Say that again," said Herbert, sternly, "and I will come ashore and give you a whipping."

"You can't do it."

"I can try."

"Don't you know I can have you arrested for stealing my boat, you loafer?"

"Who's been stealing your boat, you loafer?"

"You have."

"Are you sure of it?"

"Why, you are in my boat this very minute."

"I think you are mistaken," said Herbert, quietly.

"Don't you call that a boat you are in?"

"Yes, I do; but there's more than one boat in the world, and this isn't your boat."

He rowed near the shore as he spoke, and James, his attention drawn to the boat, saw that it wasn't his. At

The Rival Boatmen

the same time, walking nearer the edge of the pond, he caught sight of his own boat moored at its usual place.

"I guess I made a mistake," said James.

"I think you have," returned Herbert, quietly.

"Where did that boat come from?" demanded James.

"I don't know."

"You don't? Then you've taken it without leave."

"Oh, the owner won't object to my using it," said Herbert, with a queer smile.

"How do you know?"

"He's an intimate friend of mine."

"The owner?"

"Yes."

"I suppose it belongs to Mr. Cameron, then?"

"He bought it."

"Do you call him your intimate friend? He'd be proud if he heard it," said James, with a sneer.

"Would he?" said Herbert.

"I should think he would, considering your high position in society."

"I think he's a pretty good friend of mine but I have never called him an intimate friend."

"Yes, you have. You said the owner of that boat was an intimate friend of yours."

"So he is. I'm with him all the time."

"Then why do you deny that you called Mr. Cameron your intimate friend?"

"Because Mr. Cameron doesn't own the boat."

"Just now you said he bought it."

"So he did, but he doesn't own it."

"Then who does?"

"I do," was the unexpected reply.

"You—own—that—boat?" ejaculated James.

"Yes."

"Did Mr. Cameron give it to you?"

"Yes."

"I don't believe it. That boat must have cost sixty or seventy dollars. I don't believe he would give you such a present as that."

"I don't know as it makes much difference."

"When did he give it to you?"

"This afternoon. I'll row in. Perhaps you would like to examine it."

James surveyed with envious eyes the neat, graceful boat, for he saw at a glance that his own boat, even when new, was by no means its equal.

"Isn't it a beauty?" asked Herbert, not without pride.

"Very fair," answered James, condescendingly. "Did you ask Mr. Cameron to give it to you?"

"I never ask for gifts," said Herbert, with emphasis. "What makes you ask such a question as that?"

"I thought it queer that he should have given you such a handsome present."

"It was certainly very generous in him," said Herbert.

"I shouldn't think you'd want to accept it, though."

"Why not?"

"Because you are a poor boy and it don't correspond with your position."

"Perhaps not; but that don't trouble me."

"A less expensive boat would have been more appropriate."

"Perhaps it would; but you wouldn't have me refuse it on that account?"

James did not answer and Herbert asked: "Are you going out in your boat this afternoon?"

"I should like to try yours," said James.

"I shall be glad to have you," said Herbert, politely.

"And you may take mine," said James, with unwonted politeness.

"All right."

The two boys got into the boats and pulled out. James was charmed with the new boat. In every way it was superior to his own boat, apart from its being newer. It was certainly very provoking to think that a boy like Herbert Carter, poor almost to beggary, should own such a beautiful little boat, while he, a rich man's son, had to put up with an inferior one.

"I say, Herbert," he began, when they returned, "don't you want to exchange your boat for mine?"

"Not much; I should be a fool to do that."

"I don't mean even, for I know your boat is better. I'll give you five dollars to boot."

"No, thank you; there's a good deal more than five dollars' difference between your boat and mine."

"Five dollars would come handy to a poor boy like you," said James, in his usual tone of insolent condescension.

"I don't want it enough to exchange boats."

"Well, I'll give you ten dollars," said James. "That's an offer worth thinking about."

"I shan't need to think about it. I say no."

"You've got an extravagant idea of your boat. Mine is nearly as good but I've taken a fancy to yours. How will you trade, anyway?"

"I don't feel at liberty to trade at all. Mr. Cameron gave me the boat, but he is to have the use of it while he is here. He wouldn't be willing to have me exchange."

"He can have the use of it all the same if it is mine."

"It won't do, James," said Herbert, shaking his head.

"You are very foolish, then," said James, disappointed.

"I may be, but that is my answer."

James walked away. He made up his mind, since he could not have Herbert's boat, to tease his father to buy him a new one. As to rowing in an inferior one, his pride would not permit it.

CHAPTER XXVII

THE RACE

James broached the subject which was uppermost in his mind as soon as he got home.

"I wish you'd buy me a new boat, father," he said.

"What's the matter with the boat you have now?"

"I don't want to be outdone by Herbert Carter."

"I don't see how that can be."

"He's got a beautiful new boat, twice as handsome as mine ever was."

"He has!" exclaimed the squire, in amazement. "How can he have, without any money?"

"Mr. Cameron gave it to him."

"I don't believe it. Probably the boat belongs to Mr. Cameron and he has only let Herbert use it."

"No, Mr. Cameron gave it to him. Herbert told me."

"Perhaps he has not told the truth."

"He wouldn't tell a lie—that is, about that," said James, modifying his first assertion lest it might be a compliment. In reality he had implicit confidence in Herbert's word.

"You wouldn't want me to be rowing around in a poor boat, while that beggar has a new one," said James, artfully appealing to his father's pride.

"Well, the fact is, my son," said the squire, rather embarrassed, "it would not be convenient for me to buy you a new boat just now."

"Why not, father? I thought you had plenty of money."

"So I have; but I have made some investments under the advice of Mr. Temple. If you can arrange to exchange boats by paying a little to boot, you may do so."

"I have proposed it, but Herbert is very stiff about it."

"Humph!" said the squire, clearing his throat; "I think you will have to wait a while."

"How long?" asked James, dissatisfied.

"I'll tell you what I'll do," said his father. "If things go well, I expect to make a good deal of money within twelve months. Instead of a rowboat, I'll buy you a beautiful little sailboat next season."

"Will you?" exclaimed James, delighted.

"Yes; won't that be much better?"

"You are right, father."

Certainly a sailboat would be far better and there was very little chance of Herbert's having one given him. So James went out rowing contentedly the next afternoon, although Herbert was out also in the new boat.

"Your boat is better than mine," said James. "However, I am to have an elegant yacht next year."

"Are you?" said Herbert, interested.

"Father has promised to get me one. He would get me one this season but it would be some time before it could be got ready and I can have it the first thing next spring."

"I congratulate you," said Herbert. "I should like a sailboat myself."

"I dare say you would," said James, pompously, "but of course you cannot expect to have one."

"I don't think there is much chance myself, unless somebody leaves me a fortune," said Herbert, good-naturedly. "I am satisfied with this boat."

"Of course it is more than a boy in your circumstances could expect."

Herbert smiled. He was used to references to his circumstances. James never allowed him to forget that he was a poor boy. He thought it hardly worth noticing.

"Shall we have a race?" he asked.

"Just as you say," said James.

James thought himself the better rower or he would not have consented to row across the pond.

"Are you ready?" asked Herbert.

"Yes."

"Give way, then."

Both bent to their oars and rowed their best. But it was not long before Herbert began to draw away from his antagonist. He had not had as much practice as James, but he was stronger in the arms, and had paid more attention to Cameron's instructions. He came in more than a dozen lengths ahead of his competitor.

"I've won the race, James," he said, with a smile.

"You ought to," said James, in a surly tone.

"I haven't had as much practice as you."

"What if you haven't? You've got a new boat, while mine is old and clumsy."

"If you think that makes any difference I'll row back with you, changing boats."

"Agreed," said James. But James brought up the rear at about the same distance.

"Beaten again," said Herbert, pleased with his success.

"There's nothing to crow about," said James, crossly. "Your boat is a good one but I'm not used to it."

"I am not much used to it myself. I only rowed in it yesterday for the first time."

"That's long enough to get the hang of it. There isn't much fun in rowing. I'd a good deal rather sail."

"I like both. There's more exercise in rowing."

"Don't you get exercise enough in hoeing potatoes?" asked James, with a sneer. "I shouldn't think laborers would need any extra exercise."

"There's some advantage in varying your exercise. There isn't much fun in hoeing."

"No, I should think not."

"Are you going in?" asked Herbert, noticing that James was proceeding to fasten his boat.

"Yes, I've got tired of the water."

Herbert was not to be alone, however, for just then Mr. Cameron appeared on the bank.

"I think I'll go out with you," he said.

"All right," said Herbert, with alacrity, as he rowed the boat to shore.

"Mr. Cameron," said our hero, "mother has asked me to invite you to take tea with us this evening."

"I shall be very glad to come," said Cameron.

"We live in humble style, you know," said Herbert, "but I told mother you wouldn't mind that."

"Thank you for saying so. I shall be very glad to meet your mother, and expect to enjoy myself better than at Squire Leech's table. It isn't the style, but the company. Why is James going away so soon?"

"I have beaten him in two races," said Herbert.

"I am not surprised to hear of your success. You are really gaining very fast."

"I am glad of it. I want to be a good rower."

"It is a good thing to do well anything you undertake, whether it be rowing or anything else."

"James thinks I don't need to row for exercise."

"Why not?"

"He thinks I shall get enough exercise in hoeing potatoes," answered Herbert, with a smile.

"It wouldn't do him any harm to get exercise in the same way."

"The very idea would shock him."

CHAPTER XXVIII

MRS. CARTER'S GUEST

At five o'clock Mr. Cameron knocked at the door of Mrs. Carter's cottage. It was opened by Herbert himself.

"Walk in, Mr. Cameron," he said, cordially. "My mother is in the next room."

Mrs. Carter was prepossessed in favor of Cameron. In worldly advantages he was her superior; yet with the instinct of a gentleman he seemed unconscious of any such difference and did not exhibit the least trace of condescension, as many ill-bred persons might have.

"I have wanted to see you, Mrs. Carter," he said. "As the mother of my professor, the desire was only natural."

"Herbert tells me he has learned a good deal since he has been reading to you. He has often spoken of his good fortune in meeting you."

"I feel equally fortunate in meeting him. Not every boy of his age would adapt himself as readily and intelligently as he has."

"I am very glad if you find Herbert of service to you," said Mrs. Carter. "In all ways the engagement has been of advantage to him."

"Squire Leech was kind enough to offer me the services of his son, James," said Cameron, smiling.

"James would hardly have been willing to sacrifice so much of his time," said Herbert, "though he might be willing to try it for a day or two to supersede me."

"I think I shall have to worry along with my present professor," said Cameron, "and allow James to devote his superior talents to some other business."

The table was already spread in honor of the guest, and both Herbert and Mrs. Carter were gratified to find that the young collegian did ample justice to the meal.

"I feel almost ashamed of my appetite," said Cameron; "but the change from the stereotyped bill of fare at the hotel is pleasant and gives the food an increased relish."

"I am glad to hear you say so, Mr. Cameron; I could hardly expect to compete with the hotel in point of variety. Let me give you another cup of tea."

"Thank you. I don't often venture on a third cup, but I think I will make an exception to-night."

"Dr. Johnson sometimes got up to a dozen, I believe," said Herbert.

"He exceeded that number at times; but we must remember that the cups in his day barely contained a third as much as ours, so he was not so immoderate, after all. His excesses in eating were less pardonable."

"Was he a very large eater?" asked the widow.

"He actually gorged himself, if we are to believe the accounts that have come down to us," said Cameron. "I am afraid, Mrs. Carter, you would have found him a very unprofitable boarder."

"But," said Herbert; "there is one of Dr. Johnson's labors I shall not seek to imitate. I shall never attempt to write a dictionary."

"It must be a monotonous and wearisome labor. Besides, I don't think we could either of us improve upon Webster or Worcester."

They arose, and Mrs. Carter, who could not afford to keep a servant, herself cleared away the tea table.

"Herbert," said the young collegian, "you mentioned one day that your father was an inventor."

"He made one invention, but whether it will amount to anything, I don't know. He had high hopes of it, but died before he had any opportunity of testing its value."

"Will you show it to me?"

"With pleasure."

Herbert led Cameron upstairs into his own chamber, where, since his father's death, the work which had cost his father so many toilsome hours had been kept. Cameron examined it carefully. Herbert waited anxiously for his verdict. At length he spoke.

"As far as I am qualified to judge," he said, "your father's invention seems to embody an improvement. But you must not rely too much upon my opinion. My knowledge of the details of manufacturing is superficial. I should like to show it to my father."

"There is nothing that I would like better," said Herbert, "if you think he would be willing to examine it."

"He would be glad to do so. It is for his interest to examine anything which will facilitate the details of his business. I am intending to go home next Friday afternoon, and, with your permission, will carry this with me."

"I shall feel very much obliged to you if you will," said Herbert. "It may be worth nothing. I know it would have been my father's wish to have it examined by one who is qualified to judge."

"It is a pity your father could not have lived to enjoy the benefit of his invention, if it succeeds."

"He was a great loss to us," said Herbert. "There were but three of us, and he was at an age when we might hope to have him with us for a good many years yet. If I had been a few years older, I should have been better able to make up his loss to my mother."

"She is fortunate in having a son who is so willing to do his best for her," said Cameron, kindly. "We don't know what the future may have in store for us, Herbert; but you may rely upon my continued friendship."

Herbert pressed the hand of the young collegian warmly, for he knew that the offer of service was no empty compliment, but made in earnest sincerity.

The evening passed pleasantly and at nine o'clock Cameron took his leave. Herbert accompanied him as far as the hotel. He was walking leisurely back when he heard his name called and, turning, saw that it was James Leech who had accosted him.

"Where have you been, Carter?" inquired James; "been to see Mr. Cameron, I suppose? Doesn't he get enough of your company in the daytime?"

"You must ask him that. He has been taking tea at our house and I accompanied him home."

"He took supper at your house!"

"Yes."

A Bitter Pill

"He seems very fond of keeping low company."

"What do you mean?" demanded Herbert, his eyes flashing with indignation at this insolence.

"I mean what I say," answered James, doggedly.

"Then I advise you hereafter to keep your impudence to yourself," retorted Herbert; "and for fear you may forget it, I give you this as a reminder."

An instant later James Leech found himself lying on his back on the sidewalk with Herbert bending over him.

He got upon his feet, pale with rage and mortification.

"I'll be revenged upon you yet, you brute!" he shrieked, in his rage leaving our hero victor of the field.

"I wouldn't have touched him if he hadn't spoken against my mother," said Herbert.

CHAPTER XXIX

A BITTER PILL

JAMES LEECH was furious at the humiliation. What! he, a gentleman's son, to be knocked down and triumphed over by a boy who was compelled to work! Why, it was almost a sacrilege and no punishment could be too severe for such flagrant outrage. How should he be revenged? First of all, he would get Herbert discharged from his present employment. Surely Mr. Cameron would not continue to avail himself of the services of a common bully. To attain this, he decided to reveal the matter to his father.

"That boy actually knocked you down!" exclaimed the squire. "But why did you permit him?"

"He took me by surprise," said James.

"And what did you do? Did you knock him over?"

"I would," said James, "but I didn't care to pursue him. I thought I would wait and tell you."

"And what do you want me to do?"

"To get Mr. Cameron to turn him off. I want him to starve," said James, bitterly.

"You express yourself too strongly, James; but, under the circumstances, I can't blame you much. The boy is evidently a ruffian."

"Yes, he is a ruffian and a brute, and I don't see what Mr. Cameron sees about him to like, I am sure."

"Probably the boy makes him think he is a model of excellence. Such boys are apt to be deceitful."

"He's deceitful enough. You'd think butter wouldn't melt in his mouth."

"I shall make such representations to Mr. Cameron as, I flatter myself, will dispose of the case of this young rascal and make him repent his brutal and unprovoked assault. I'll go over to-morrow forenoon to the hotel and speak to him on the subject," said the squire, pompously.

"Thank you, father. Put it as strong as you can."

"I will, you may be assured of that."

"If I can only get him turned off, I won't mind his hitting me," thought James. "I hope to see him in the penitentiary some day. It would do him good."

It so happened that Cameron had met Herbert in a walk he took before breakfast and had been informed of the occurrence of the evening previous.

"I don't know whether I ought to have struck James," said Herbert, in conclusion; "but when he called my mother and myself low, I couldn't help it."

"I am glad you did it," said the young collegian. "The boy is a disagreeable cub and deserves more than one lesson of that sort. Didn't he offer to hit you back?"

"No."

"So I supposed. I don't approve of fighting; but if he had shown a little courage to back his insolence, I should have despised him less. What will he do?"

"He will injure me, if he can," said Herbert.

"We will see what comes of it. Meanwhile, in this matter, you may count upon my support."

Herbert thanked his friend, not realizing how likely Cameron was to be called upon to redeem his promise.

Shortly after breakfast, Cameron was told that Squire Leech wished to see him.

"Good-morning, Mr. Cameron," said the squire. "This is an early call."

"Not too early, sir," said the young collegian.

"The fact is, I have called on unpleasant business."

"Really, sir, I am sorry to hear it."

"It is about the Carter boy who is in your employ."

"By the Carter boy, you mean my young friend, Herbert Carter, I suppose," said Cameron, significantly.

"Of course if you choose to regard him as a friend."

"I certainly do."

"I don't think you will look upon him in that light when you hear that last evening he brutally assaulted my son James, without provocation, in the village street, taking him by surprise and knocking him over."

Cameron did not seem as much shocked as the squire anticipated. He took the revelation very coolly.

"You say he did this without provocation?"

"Yes, Mr. Cameron."

"Did James tell you this?"

"He did; and he is a boy of truth."

"But perhaps he did not look upon it as a provocation when he called Herbert and his mother low."

"He didn't say anything about that."

"I dare say not."

"And even if he did use the word, it would not justify Carter in brutally assaulting him."

"I confess I don't agree with you there, Squire Leech. I hate brutality as much as anyone and an unprovoked assault I certainly look upon as brutal. But for a boy to resent an insult directed against his mother is quite a different matter, and if Herbert had not acted as he did, I should have been ashamed of him."

Squire Leech flushed all over his face. This certainly was plain speaking.

"You have probably been misled by Carter's statement. I don't believe my boy did anything, or said anything, that Carter had a right to complain of."

"From what I have observed of your son, I regret to differ with you."

"You are prejudiced against James."

"I was not to begin with; but what I have seen of him, certainly, has not prepossessed me in his favor. He seems disposed to be insolent to those whom he fancies beneath him in social position."

"If you refer to the Carter boy," said the squire, pompously, "I should say that James is right in regarding him as a social inferior."

"I won't argue that point, or consider how far the possession of money, which is certainly the only point in which Herbert is inferior, justifies your son in looking down upon him. I will only say that he has no right to insult his social inferiors."

The discussion had assumed such a different character from what the squire anticipated, that he found it difficult to come to the request he had in view. But he did it.

"I am certainly astonished, Mr. Cameron, to find you so prejudiced against my son. If you should find you had done him an injustice, and that the Carter boy was really the aggressor last evening, will you be willing to discharge him from your employment?"

"If I find Herbert justifies your denunciations and his assault was unprovoked, I will discharge him."

"Then you can do it at once. You have my son's word for it."

"And I have Herbert's word for the contrary."

"Between the two, I believe James."

"Does James deny that he called Herbert and his mother low?"

"I have not asked him."

"If you will do so and bring me his assurance that he said nothing of the kind, I will examine Herbert again and try to get at the truth."

"Very well; I will put the question to him."

Squire Leech did so on his return home.

"I don't know but I called him something of the kind," James admitted; "but it's true, isn't it?"

"As to that, the boy certainly acted in a very low manner. But you shouldn't have called him so."

"I couldn't help it, when I heard him boasting of Mr. Cameron's having taken supper at his house. Won't Cameron discharge him?"

"No," said the squire, shortly; "he is infatuated about that boy."

"Suppose we cut both of them?"

"It won't do, James. Mr. Cameron's father is a wealthy manufacturer—much richer than I am. We must keep on good terms with him, but we needn't notice the Carter boy. Some day he and his mother will be in my power."

"I hope so, father. I want to bring him to his knees, the proud beggar!"

It was a bitter pill for James to swallow, seeing his rival high in the favor of the young collegian.

CHAPTER XXX

OUT OF WORK AGAIN

Mr. Cameron went home on Friday afternoon.

"I shall be back Monday night," he said to Herbert.

But Monday night did not bring him. Herbert didn't think much of it, however, as it was easy to imagine that some engagement had delayed the young collegian. Tuesday morning, however, he received a letter from Cameron, which contained unexpected and unwelcome intelligence. It ran thus:

"My Dear Herbert: When I left you, I fully expected to return on Monday, but an unexpected proposal has been made to me, which I think it expedient to accept. The physician whom I consulted about my eyes recommends a sea voyage as likely to benefit me, and advises me to start at once. A fellow student is intending to sail on Saturday next for Rio Janeiro, and I have decided to go with him. While I hope to reap advantage from the voyage, I regret that our pleasant intimacy should terminate so suddenly. I ought not to use the word 'terminate,' however, as I fully intend to keep track of you, if I can, in your future plans. I may be gone some months, perhaps a year, but when I return I shall manage to meet you.

"I have submitted your father's invention to my father, who will examine it when he has leisure, and communicate with you. There may be some delay, as he is obliged to go to Europe for three months on business.

"I am owing you five dollars, but inclose fifteen, which I beg you to accept, with my thanks for your services, and my best wishes for your happiness and prosperity."

This was the letter which Herbert read with feelings of regret, almost bordering upon dismay. He missed the daily companionship of Cameron, for whom he had formed an attachment almost brotherly, and, besides, he was forced to regard the departure of his friend in its bearing upon his material interests. The income upon which he chiefly depended was suddenly withdrawn, and, look where he might, he could not see where he was to supply the deficiency. The fifteen dollars which Cameron had so considerately sent him would, indeed, last some time; but when that was spent what was he to do? This was a question which cost him anxious thought.

It was not till the day afterward that James Leech heard of Cameron's departure. It is needless to say that he took a malicious satisfaction in the thought that his enemy would now be deprived of his main income. He hastened to inform his father.

"What? Cameron gone away? That is unexpected," said the squire.

"Yes; it is sudden."

"Where is he gone?"

"They told me at the hotel that he was going to sail to South America. His eyes are weak, you know, and the doctor thinks the voyage will do him good."

"I wonder he didn't take the Carter boy with him; he seemed infatuated with him."

"He don't care anything about Carter. At any rate, he will forget all about him, now he is away. The beggarly upstart will have to draw in his horns now. He won't put on so many airs, I'm thinking."

"How much did Cameron pay him for reading to him?"

"Five dollars a week."

"A perfectly preposterous price."

"So I think. But he won't get it now."

"They'll find it hard to get along."

"Of course they will. They can't pay you interest on the mortgage now."

"I don't see how they can."

"And you can take possession of the house, can't you?"

"I certainly shall if the interest isn't paid promptly."

"Perhaps Carter would sell his boat now. He was pretty stiff about it before."

"I wouldn't make him an offer."

"Why not?"

"If he succeeded in selling the boat he might be able to pay the interest, and delay my getting possession of the property."

"That is true," said James. "I didn't think of that. Besides, you have promised me a sailboat next spring."

"If business is good, as I hope it may be, you shall have one. At present I am rather short of money."

"I thought you always had plenty of money, father," said James, in surprise.

"I have been buying stocks in the city, James, and that has tied up my money. However, I shall probably make a very handsome profit when I sell out. My friend assures me that I stand a chance of making twenty thousand dollars," concluded the squire, complacently.

"That's a big pile of money," said James. "Are you pretty sure of making it?"

"The chances are greatly in my favor. Of course, it depends on the turn of the market."

"If you succeed, will you move to New York, father?"

"Very probably."

"I hope you will. This village is awfully slow. New York is the place to see life."

"There are some kinds of life it is not profitable to see," said the squire, shrewdly.

"I don't want to be cooped up in a little country village all my life," grumbled James.

"You won't be. Don't trouble yourself on that score."

"It will do well enough for Carter. He isn't fit for anything but a country bumpkin, but it don't suit me."

"Well, James, you must be patient, and things may turn out as you desire."

At the same time Herbert was holding a consultation with his mother.

"My prospects are not very bright here, mother," he said, rather despondently. "I am ready enough to work, but there is no work to be had, so far as I can see."

Out of Work Again

"You forget your garden, Herbert."

"Yes; that will help us a little; but I can't expect to clear more than twenty dollars out of it, and twenty dollars won't go a great way."

"It is something, Herbert."

"It isn't enough to pay our next interest bill."

Mrs. Carter looked troubled.

"If I could sell the property for what it cost your father I should be tempted to do it."

"You mean for fifteen hundred dollars?"

"Yes; that would give us seven hundred and fifty dollars over the mortgage."

"I should be in favor of selling, too, in that case; but Squire Leech only offers eleven hundred at the outside."

"He ought to be more considerate."

"He wants to make a bargain at your expense, mother. That isn't all. He is provoked to think you haven't accepted his offer before, and, of course, that won't incline him to be any more liberal."

"I am afraid we shall have to part with our home," said the widow, with a sigh.

"There is one hope, mother. I don't like to think of it too much, for fear it won't amount to anything; but father's invention may prove valuable. You know Mr. Cameron's father has agreed to examine it."

"If we could only get two or three hundred dollars for it, it would be a great help."

"If we get anything at all we shall get more. I am afraid we shall have to wait, though, for Mr. Cameron writes me his father is going to Europe for a few months."

"Everything seems against us, Herbert," said his mother, in a despondent tone.

But Herbert was more hopeful.

"If we can only manage to keep along and pay the next interest, I think we'll be all right, mother," he said. "I mean to try, anyway. If there's any work to be had anywhere within five miles, I'll try to obtain it. How much money have you got left, mother?"

"Ten dollars and a half."

"And here are fifteen that Mr. Cameron sent me. No chance of the poorhouse for a month, mother. Before that has gone by something may turn up."

CHAPTER XXXI

A NEW START

HARVEST came, and for the time Herbert was busy. He could not afford to hire assistance, and was obliged to do all the work himself. When all was finished, and his share of the vegetables sold, he sat down to count up his profits.

"Well, mother," he asked, "how much money do you think I have made by farming?"

"You expected to make twenty dollars."

"I have cleared twenty-one dollars and a half besides the vegetables I have brought home and stored in the cellar."

"That is doing very well," said Mrs. Carter.

"I have had to work very hard for it," said Herbert, thoughtfully, "and for a good many days. After all, it isn't quite enough to pay our interest."

"The interest doesn't come due for six weeks yet."

"That is true, mother; but six weeks hence we shall be poorer than we are now. We shall have to use some of this money for current expenses, and I know of no way to replace it."

"You may earn some more."

"I don't see any chance—that is, here. There is nothing doing in Wrayburn. If there were any factories or workshops, I might stand a chance of getting something to do."

Mrs. Carter did not reply. She knew that Herbert was right, and she had nothing to suggest.

"I have thought of something," said Herbert; "but you may not like it at first."

"What is it?" asked his mother, with interest.

"Would you have any objection to my going to New York and trying my fortune there?"

Mrs. Carter uttered a little cry of dismay.

"You go to New York—a boy of your age!" she exclaimed.

"I am old enough to take care of myself," said Herbert, sturdily.

"A great city is a dangerous place."

"It won't be dangerous for me. I shall be too busy—that is, if I get work—to fall into temptation, if that is what you mean."

"I should miss you so much, Herbert, even if I knew you were doing well," said his mother, pathetically.

"I know you would, mother; and I should miss you, too; but I can't live here always. If I do well in the city you can come and join me there."

This was the first time Herbert broached the subject of going to New York. He resumed the attack the next day, and the next, and finally won his mother's consent to go for a week, and see whether he could find anything to do.

His mother's consent obtained, Herbert took but a day to make his preparations. The next day, after an early breakfast, he started for the great city, excited with the idea of going, but hardly able to repress the tears as he saw the lonely look upon his mother's face.

He was her only son, and she was a widow.

"I must send her good news as soon as possible," he thought. "That will cheer her up."

About noon Herbert reached the city. He had formed no particular plan, except to find Cornelius Dixon, who would doubtless be able to advise him about getting a place, perhaps would have influence enough to procure him one. He did not know where to look for Cornelius, but concluded that his name would be in the city directory. He entered a small liquor store, which he happened to pass, and walked up to the counter.

"Good-morning," said he politely, addressing a young man behind the bar.

This young man had coarse red hair, and a mottled complexion, and looked as if he patronized freely the liquors he sold. He turned his glance upon Herbert, who stood before him with his fresh, inquiring face, holding under his arm a small bundle of clothing tied up in a paper.

"Hello, yourself!" he answered. "Want some bitters?"

"Thank you," said Herbert, innocently, "I don't require any medicine."

"Medicine?" repeated the other, with a frown. "Do you mean to compare my drinks to medicine?"

"You said bitters," returned Herbert.

"You're from the country, ain't you?" asked the bartender.

"Yes, sir."

"So I thought. You haven't cut your eyeteeth yet. When a gentleman takes a drink he takes his bitters. Now, what'll you have?"

"Nothing, thank you."

"Oh, you needn't thank me. I didn't offer to give you a drink. What do you want, anyhow?"

"Have you got a directory?"

"No; we don't keep one. We don't care where our customers live. All we want is their money."

Herbert did not fancy the bartender's tone or manner; but felt that it would be foolish to get angry. So he explained: "I have a cousin living in the city; I thought I could find out where he lived in the directory."

"What's your cousin's name?"

"Cornelius Dixon."

"Never heard of him. He don't buy his bitters at this shop."

It was clear that no satisfaction was to be found here, and Herbert looked further. Finally, at a druggist's he found a directory, and hopefully looked for the name. But another disappointment awaited him. There were several Dixons, but Cornelius was not among them.

"I must give him up, and see what I can do by myself," thought Herbert. "I wish I could come across him."

It seemed strange to him that one who was so prominent as Cornelius claimed to be, and who had been living for years in the city, should have been overlooked by the compilers of the directory. He was not discouraged, however; he expected to encounter difficulties, and this was the first one.

He kept on his way, attracting some attention as he walked. The city Arab knows a stranger by instinct.

"Carry your bundle, mister?" asked a ragged urchin.

"No; thank you. I can carry it myself."

"I won't charge you much. Take you to any hotel in the city."

"I don't think I shall go to any hotel. I can't afford it. Can you show me a cheap boarding house?"

"Yes," said the boy. "What'll you give?"

"Ten cents."

"That ain't enough. It wouldn't keep me in cigars an hour."

"Do you smoke?" asked Herbert, surprised.

"In course I do. I've smoked for four or five years."

"How old are you?"

"The old woman says I'm ten. She ought to know."

"It isn't good for boys to smoke," said Herbert, gravely.

"Oh, bosh! Dry up! All us boys smoke."

Herbert felt that his advice was not called for, and he came to business.

"I'll give you fifteen cents," he said, "if you'll show me a good, cheap boarding house."

"Well," said the Arab, "business is poor, and I'll do it for once. Come along."

Herbert concluded from the boy's appearance that he would be more likely to know of cheap than of fashionable boarding houses; but it did not occur to him that there was such a thing as being too cheap. He realized it when the boy brought him to the door of a squalid dwelling in a filthy street, and, pointing to it, complacently remarked: "That's the place you want—that's Rafferty's."

Herbert stared at it in dismay. Accustomed to the utmost neatness, he was appalled at the idea of lodging in such a place.

"Gimme them fifteen cents, mister," said the boy, impatiently.

"But I don't like the place. I wouldn't stay here."

"It's cheap," said the young Arab. "Rafferty'll give you a lodging for ten cents, meals fifteen. You can't complain of that, now."

"I don't complain of the price. It's dirty. I wouldn't stay in such a dirty place."

"Oh, you're a fine gentleman, you are!" said the boy, sarcastically. "You'd better go to the Fifth Avenoo Hotel, you had."

"I won't stop here. I want some decent place."

Meanwhile, Mrs. Rafferty herself had come to the door, and caught the meaning of the conference. She took instant umbrage at Herbert's last words.

"Dacent, do ye say?" she repeated, with flaming eyes and arms akimbo. "Who dares to say that Bridget Rafferty doesn't keep a dacent house?"

"He does," said the Arab, indicating Herbert, with a grin.

"And who are you, I'd like to know?" demanded Mrs. Rafferty, turning upon Herbert angrily. "Who are you, that talks agin' a poor widder that's tryin' to earn an honest living?"

"I beg your pardon, madam," said Herbert, anxious to get out of the scrape. "I meant no offense."

"Lucky for you, thin!" said Mrs. Rafferty, in a belligerent tone. "Be off wid you both, thin, or I'll call a cop."

Herbert turned to go, nothing loath, but his guide followed him.

"Gimme them fifteen cents," he demanded.

"You haven't shown me a good boarding place."

"Yes, I did."

"You don't seem to know what I want. I'll give you five cents, and look out for myself."

The young Arab tried for ten; but Herbert was firm. He felt that he had no money to waste, and that he had selected a poor guide. It was wiser to rely upon himself.

CHAPTER XXXII

OPENING THE CAMPAIGN

Not knowing his way, but wandering wherever the fancy seized him, Herbert finally came to Washington Square, and took a seat on one of the benches provided for the public. He looked around him with interest, surveying the groups that passed him, though without the expectation of recognizing anyone. But, as good fortune would have it, the very person he most desired to see strolled by.

Mr. Cornelius Dixon looked like a cheap swell. In his dress he caricatured the fashion, and exhibited a sort of pretentious gentility which betrayed his innate vulgarity. He stared in wonder when a boy with a bundle under his arm started from his seat, and hurried toward him with the greeting: "How do you do, Mr. Dixon?"

"Really," drawled Cornelius, "you have the advantage of me."

"Don't you remember me? I am your cousin, Herbert Carter."

"What! the boy the old fellow left his old clothes to?" asked Cornelius.

"The same one," answered Herbert, smiling.

"You haven't got any of 'em on, have you?" asked Mr. Dixon, surveying him with curiosity.

"Yes; this coat was made from my uncle's cloak."

"Shouldn't have thought it. It looks quite respectable, 'pon my honor. When did you come to the city?"

"Only this morning."

"On a visit?"

"No; I want to find a place."

"Humph!" muttered Cornelius, thoughtfully. "Places don't grow on every bush. Where are you hanging out?"

"I haven't found a place yet. I want to find a cheap boarding house."

"You might come to mine."

"Perhaps you pay more than I could afford," suggested Herbert, who was not aware that Cornelius had a very limited income, and occupied a room on the fourth floor of a Bleecker Street boarding house, at the weekly expense of five dollars.

"You can come into my room for a day or two, and then we'll see what arrangement we can make. I'm going there now. Will you come along?"

Herbert gladly accepted the invitation. He was tired of wandering about the great city, not knowing where to lay his head; accordingly he joined his genteel cousin, and they walked toward Bleecker Street.

"Have you got any money?" queried Cornelius, cautiously.

"Not much. If I don't find something to do in a week, I must go back to the country."

"A week's a short time to find a place. But hold on! We want a boy in our store. I guess I could get you in."

"What wages would I get?"

"Two dollars a week, to begin with."

"I couldn't live on that, could I?"

"I guess not. Four dollars a week would be the least you could get boarded for."

"Then it will be better for me to go home than to stay here, and get into debt."

"Perhaps it would," said Cornelius, who was afraid Herbert might want to borrow of him.

"Can't I get something better? How much do you get?"

"Ahem! only twenty dollars a week," answered Mr. Dixon, who really got about half that.

"Why, that's splendid!" said Herbert.

"So it would be if I only got it," thought Cornelius. "I can't save anything," he answered. "I have to dress in the fashion, you know, on account of my position in society."

Herbert privately thought, from an inspection of his cousin's wardrobe, that the fashion was a queer one, but he did not say so.

"It's a shame the old man didn't leave us more," said Mr. Dixon, in an aggrieved tone.

"It would have been convenient," Herbert admitted.

"He ought to have left us ten thousand dollars apiece."

"What would you have done with so much money?"

"Gone into business on my own account. If I had a store of my own I might have offered you a place."

"But suppose I had ten thousand dollars, too?"

"Then I would have taken you into partnership. It would be a grand thing for you to be junior partner in a New York firm."

Herbert thought so, too, though it is doubtful whether a firm of which Mr. Dixon was the head would have occupied so proud a position as some others.

"I suppose you have spent all your legacy?" said Herbert.

"I should say so. What's a hundred dollars? I bought a new suit of clothes, a dozen pair of kids, and a box of cigars, and that took up about all of it. You don't smoke, do you?"

"Oh, no," answered Herbert, surprised at the question.

"Better not. It's expensive. Wait a minute. I want to buy a cigar."

Mr. Dixon dove into a cigar store, and emerged with one in his mouth.

Soon they reached the boarding house. It was a five-story brick building, rather shabby outwardly.

Cornelius opened the door with a night key, and bade Herbert follow. So he did, up to the fifth floor, where his guide opened a door and admitted him into a room about ten feet square, in a bad state of disorder. In the corner was a bed, not very inviting in appearance. It looked very different from the neat little bed which Herbert slept in at home. The furniture was of hair, and had evidently seen better days. There were two chairs, both of them covered with portions of Mr. Dixon's wardrobe. Cornelius cleared off one, and invited Herbert to be seated.

"This is my den," he said.

"Den," seemed to be the right word, though Herbert did not say so. He wondered why a man with so large an income did not live better.

"You can brush your hair if you want to," said Cornelius. "The supper bell will ring right off. I'll take you down with me."

"Will there be room?" asked Herbert.

"Oh, yes; I'll arrange about that. If you like you can room with me, and I guess I can fix it so you needn't pay

Opening the Campaign

more than four dollars a week, getting your lunch outside."

"I wish you would," said Herbert, who felt that, dirty as the room was, it would be more like home to him than where he was wholly unacquainted.

At the table below, Herbert found a seat next to Cornelius. There were other clerks at the table whom Mr. Dixon knew, also two or three married couples, and two extra ladies.

"That lady is an actress," whispered Cornelius, pointing to a rather faded woman, of about thirty, on the opposite side of the table.

"Is she?" returned Herbert, examining her with considerable curiosity. "Where does she play?"

"At the Olympic," said Mr. Dixon. "She is Rosalie Vernon."

"That's a pretty name."

"It's only her stage name. Her real name is Brown."

"Did you ever see her play?"

"Often; she's good."

"She looks very quiet."

"She don't say much here; but on the stage she has enough to say for herself. Do you see that man with gray hair and spectacles?"

"Yes."

"He's an Italian count. He lost his property somehow, and is obliged to give lessons in French and Italian. Quite a come-down, isn't it?"

In the evening he discussed his plans with Cornelius.

"Can't I get more than two dollars a week in a store?" he asked.

"I am afraid not; though you might stumble on a place where they would give three."

"Even that would not be enough to live upon. I must make that, at any rate, and I hoped to be able to save something."

"There are some newsboys who make a dollar a day," suggested Cornelius.

"A dollar a day? That's six dollars a week."

"Exactly."

"Do you think I could go into that?"

"Of course you can, if you've got money enough to buy a stock of papers to start with. You'll be your own boss. Then there's bootblacking; but that ain't genteel."

"I should prefer selling papers."

"Then you'd better try it. I've spoken to the landlady, and she'll take you for four dollars a week."

Herbert closed the day in good spirits. He thought he saw his way clear to supporting himself in the city. Before he went to bed he wrote a cheerful letter to his mother and deposited it in a post office box at the corner.

CHAPTER XXXIII

HERBERT AS A NEWSBOY

THE next morning, by advice of his roommate, Herbert got up early, and made his way downtown and obtained a supply of morning papers.

The first day was not a success, chiefly on account of his inexperience. He was "stuck" on nearly half his papers, and the profits were less than nothing. But Herbert was quick to learn. The second day, though he still had some papers left, he cleared twenty-five cents. The third day he netted seventy-five. He felt now that he had passed the period of experiment, and that he would at any rate, be able to pay his board. Of course, he hoped for something better, and indeed felt confident of it.

Three weeks later, about eleven o'clock in the forenoon, as he stood in front of the Astor House, with his last paper in his hand, he heard his name called:

"Hello, Carter; are you here?"

He did not need to turn around to recognize James Leech.

"Good-morning, James," he said, politely.

"So you're a newsboy," said James.

"Yes; any way to make a living."

"Do you make much?" inquired his old foe, curiously.

"I haven't made enough to retire upon yet; but I can manage to pay my board."

"How much do you pay for your board?"

Herbert hesitated about gratifying his curiosity, but finally did so.

"Four dollars," repeated James, scornfully. "It can't be much of a boarding house."

"An Italian count boards there," said Herbert, knowing James' respect for rank.

"You don't say so!" returned James, rather impressed. "Did he ever speak to you?"

"He spoke to me this morning."

"What did he say?"

"'Will you pass ze butter?'"

"Do you save up any money?" inquired James.

Herbert penetrated his motive in asking the question, and did not mean to give too definite information. But James was bent on learning all he could.

"How much do you make a day?" he asked.

"Sometimes more, sometimes less, just as it happens."

"I can't tell anything from that."

"Why do you want to know?" asked Herbert, pointedly.

"Curiosity, I suppose."

"So I thought. If it was from interest in me, I would tell you; but I don't care to gratify your curiosity."

"You don't expect me to feel any interest in a common newsboy, do you?"

"No; I don't. I know you too well for that."

"I don't see what object you have in refusing to answer my questions."

"If you are thinking of going into the business, yourself, I'll tell you."

"I a newsboy? I sell papers in the street? You must be crazy!" returned James, haughtily.

"I suppose you feel above it," said Herbert, smiling.

"To be sure I do. Haven't I a right to?"

"Oh, you must settle that question for yourself. Papers, sir?"

The gentleman addressed purchased the last remaining paper, and Herbert was free till afternoon.

"How do you like the city?" asked James.

"Very much. I should like to have my mother here; then I would be contented."

"We may come to live here," said James. "Of course, we shall live in a brownstone front, uptown."

"I live in a brick house," said Herbert, smiling.

"Fashionable people live in brownstone fronts."

"I may be rich some time."

"Then you'll have to go into some other business. But there isn't much hope for you. You'll be a poor man."

"You seem very confident of it."

"You've got no chance, you know. But I must be going."

"Who do you think I met this morning, father?" asked James, later in the day.

"I don't know."

"The Carter boy."

"Where did you meet him?"

"He was selling papers in front of the Astor House."

"He won't get rich very fast in that business. What did he have to say for himself?"

"He wouldn't tell me how much money he was making. He pays four dollars a week for board."

"He probably finds it hard to pay that. It isn't likely

he lays up anything. He would do better to stay in Wrayburn."

"Then you think he can't send any money to his mother?"

"No; he will find it hard to pay his own expenses."

"Then she won't be able to pay the interest on the mortgage?"

"I don't see how she can."

"And you will seize the house?"

"I fully intend to do so."

"Good! That'll bring down Carter's pride. He's as cheeky as ever."

"He hasn't much to be proud of."

"That don't seem to make any difference with him. He talks as if he were my equal."

"That don't make him so."

"When are you going to move to the city, father?"

"I don't know," said the squire, shortly.

"I've got tired of Wrayburn."

"You'll have to stay there till my business will allow me to move."

The fact was, Squire Leech had just had an unsatisfactory interview with Mr. Andrew Temple. Under the advice of that gentleman he had invested a very considerable sum of money in some mining shares, in the assurance that he would be able in a very short time to sell at a large profit. But from the time he bought, they began to drop. He asked an explanation of Mr. Temple.

"My dear sir," said the financier, "there's no being sure of the market. So many trivial circumstances affect it, that the wisest of us cannot absolutely predict anything. We can only calculate probabilities."

"You told me there was no doubt about the stock rising," grumbled the squire.

"Nor is there any, if you only have patience to wait. Rome was not built in a day, you know."

"It seems to me there is a good deal of uncertainty and risk in these stock operations," objected the squire, very sensibly.

"Not under discreet guidance; if you only have pluck and patience, you are morally sure of a fortune in the end. Fortunes are made every day. Why, there's old Jenkins, a grocer on Sixth Avenue—you've heard of his luck, haven't you?"

"No."

"Made fifty thousand dollars in six months from an original investment of ten thousand. At first, things went against him, but he was bound to see the thing through, and he did, and he's forty thousand better off for it."

"What did he invest in?" asked the squire, eagerly.

Mr. Temple told him, but I regret to say that the whole thing was a fiction, intended to encourage his dupe. He succeeded in influencing the squire to put another large sum into his hands, and sent him away hopeful. To raise this sum Squire Leech was obliged to sell or mortgage most of his real estate to parties whom Mr. Temple found for him. The prices realized were less than his valuation of the property; but Temple told him this was not so important, as he was sure to double his money in twelve months by investments in Wall Street.

So Squire Leech gave himself up to dreams of sudden wealth. He subscribed for two financial papers, and spent many hours in studying their columns. He was soon able to talk glibly of stocks and bonds, and the Wrayburn people thought he was on the high road to becoming a millionaire.

"Depend upon it, the squire's a long-headed man," said old Tom Cooper, in the village tavern. "It wouldn't surprise me a mite if he died worth a million."

CHAPTER XXXIV

HERBERT'S LEGACY

The weeks slipped rapidly away. Herbert succeeded in maintaining himself at his new business, and never failed to have ready the four dollars which he had agreed to pay for board. It was lucky he did, for he soon found that there would be no chance of borrowing from his roommate. Cornelius was always hard up. As he only paid a dollar more board than Herbert, the latter wondered what he did with his twenty dollars a week. But the fact was, Mr. Dixon at present received but half that sum, though pride induced him to represent otherwise. And what, I ask, are ten dollars a week to a young man of fashionable tastes? No wonder he was always short of funds. How could it be otherwise?

Of course it was satisfactory to Herbert to feel that he was paying his way. But still he had a source of anxiety. He felt that he ought—indeed, it was absolutely necessary—to contribute to his mother's support. Moreover, the dreaded day on which the semi-annual interest came due was now close at hand. So far as he could judge, his mother would have nothing to meet it. It seemed inevitable that she should submit to the squire's demand, and sacrifice the house. It was a sad thing to think of, yet there was this consolation: the three or four hundred dollars cash which the squire would pay would tide over the next year or two, until Herbert was older and could earn more.

But, after all, was it certain that he would earn more? Could he sell more papers two years hence than now? That was hardly likely. If he wanted to advance his income, it must be in some other business. Yet, to a boy situated as he was, there was little chance of getting any employment that would make as good immediate returns as selling papers.

So, thinking over these things, our hero was much perplexed, and could see no way out of the difficulty. He had never read "David Copperfield," and had not accustomed himself to expecting something to turn up. He was sensible enough, indeed, to know that it is idle to wait for such chances. Yet, when one does his duty faithfully, things will occasionally turn up, and this was precisely what happened to Herbert.

He was standing at his accustomed post one day, when a pleasant-looking gentleman of fifty, or perhaps a little more, accosted him, inquiring for a particular morning paper.

"I haven't got it, sir; but I will get you one," said Herbert.

"Will you be long?"

"No, sir; I know where I can get one at once."

"Very well, then, I will wait here till you return."

Herbert was as good as his word. As the gentleman paid him, he asked, pleasantly: "How is business, my young friend?"

"Pretty good, sir."

"Can you make money enough to support yourself?"

"Yes, sir."

"Then I suppose you are contented?"

"I should be, sir, if I had only myself to look after."

"You haven't a wife and family, I presume," said the gentleman, smiling.

Herbert laughed.

"I hope not yet, sir," he answered. "But I have a mother whom I ought to assist."

"And you cannot?"

"I have not been able to yet. It takes all I can earn to pay my own expenses."

"Does your mother live in the city?"

"No, sir; in the town of Wrayburn, fifty or sixty miles from here."

"Wrayburn?" repeated the gentleman, in surprise.

"Yes, sir; it is a small village. I dare say you never heard of it."

"But I have heard of it. My son passed a few weeks there during the last summer."

It was Herbert's turn to be surprised. He examined the gentleman's face attentively, and it dawned upon him who he was.

"Are you Mr. Cameron?" he asked.

"How is it that you know me?" inquired the other.

"My name is Herbert Carter. I was employed to read to your son. Have you heard from him?"

"We are expecting a letter daily, but the distance is considerable, and we may have to wait for some time yet. So you are Herbert Carter?"

"Yes, sir."

"My son was very much interested in you. He has spoken often of you."

"He was very kind to me."

"Your father was an inventor."

"That was not his business, but he devoted his leisure to invention."

"My son placed in my hands, for examination, a model of his, just before he went away."

"Have you examined it? What do you think of it, sir?" asked Herbert, eagerly.

"I only recently returned from Europe, and have not thoroughly examined it. So far as I have done so, I am inclined to think favorably of it."

Herbert's heart bounded with hope.

"Do you think we can get anything for it?" he asked.

"I think you can. Indeed, if further examination bears out my first favorable impressions, I will myself make you an offer for it."

"I should be so glad, for mother's sake!" exclaimed Herbert.

"My young friend," said Mr. Cameron, "I like your feeling toward your mother. I sincerely hope I may be able to make you a satisfactory offer. By the way, how are you situated? Can you leave the city this afternoon?"

"Yes, sir."

"Then come home with me. You shall be my guest for a week. During that time we will examine and decide about the model."

"Thank you, sir; you are very kind," said Herbert, hesitating.

"What makes you hesitate?"

"I am afraid I don't look fit to visit a gentleman's family."

"Oh, never mind that," said Mr. Cameron, heartily. "We are plain people, and don't value fine dress."

"Will there be time for me to go home first?"

"Yes; you can meet me two hours hence at the St. Nicholas Hotel. I occupy Room 121. On second thoughts, you may as well wait for me in the reading room."

"All right, sir."

Herbert hurried home, arrayed himself in clean clothes, put up a small bundle of necessary articles, and in an hour and a half was at the hotel awaiting Mr. Cameron. He left a note for Cornelius Dixon, explaining that he was called out of the city for a few days, but would write soon. He did not enter into details, for he was not at all certain that things would turn out as he hoped.

Mr. Cameron lived in a substantial country house, with a fine garden attached. Nothing was wanting of comfort in his hospitable home, but he avoided show and ostentation. To Herbert was assigned a large, well-furnished chamber, the best he had ever occupied, and he was made

Herbert's Legacy

to feel at home. The next day he accompanied Mr. Cameron to the manufactory, which he found to be a scene of busy industry, employing three hundred hands.

"I shall be busy to-day; but to-night I will look at your father's model," said the manufacturer. "Probably it will be three or four days before I can come to any decision."

Herbert passed his time pleasantly for the next three or four days. Yet he could not avoid feeling anxious. Interest day was close at hand, and his hopes might end in failure.

On the fourth day Mr. Cameron said to him: "Well, Herbert, I have made up my mind about your father's invention."

Herbert's suspense was great. His heart almost stopped beating.

The manufacturer went on:

"I consider it practicable, and am disposed to make you an offer for it. Are you authorized to conclude terms?"

"My mother will agree to anything I propose, sir."

"Then this is my offer. The model must be patented at once. I will see to that. Then make over to me half the invention, and I will agree to pay you and your mother one thousand dollars a year for the next ten years."

"Are you in earnest?" gasped Herbert.

"Entirely so," said Mr. Cameron. "Will that satisfy you?"

"I would have accepted a quarter of the sum you offer, sir."

"Better not tell me that," said Mr. Cameron, smiling. "I might take advantage of it. Will you consider it a bargain, then?"

"Oh, how happy my mother will be!" said Herbert.

"Don't you want to go home, and carry the news?"

"I should like to very much."

Then his countenance changed. Two days hence, as he

reflected, the interest would be payable. Must they lose the house, after all? If only he had a small part of the money, it would make matters all right.

"Does anything trouble you?" asked the manufacturer, noticing the sudden change in his countenance.

Upon this Herbert told him exactly how they were situated in regard to the house, and in what danger they were of losing it.

"If it's nothing worse that that," said Mr. Cameron, cheerfully, "you needn't feel anxious. I will advance you a hundred dollars on account of the contract, and you shall give me a receipt for it."

Herbert's face cleared instantly, and he was warm in his gratitude.

The next morning he started for home.

After all, the little model which his father left behind had proved to be his most valuable legacy.

CHAPTER XXXV

HERBERT'S RETURN

Mrs. Carter was setting the table for her solitary supper. She had been very lonely since Herbert went away. The days seemed doubly long. Most of all she missed him at mealtime. He kept her informed of all that was going on in the village, and when there was no news to tell he talked over their plans for the future. Life seemed very dull and monotonous without him. Yet the poor mother always wrote cheerfully, for she did not want to damp his courage, or interfere with the plan of life he had formed. She felt that there was nothing for him to do in Wrayburn, and, since she could not go to him, they must be content to live apart for the present.

"I wish I could see my boy," she sighed, as she poured

out her solitary cup of tea, and tried to force down a few mouthfuls of toast. " Shall we ever be able to live together again? "

There was a noise at the outer door, a quick step was heard, and Herbert rushed in, nearly upsetting the table in his impetuosity, as he embraced his mother.

" Are you glad to see me, mother? " he asked.

" You don't know how I have longed to see you! " was the heartfelt reply.

She did not ask what brought him home, nor care to ask just yet. She was too happy in having him back.

" You don't ask for my news, mother," said Herbert, after a pause.

" Is it good news? " she asked, wistfully.

" Suppose I should tell you that Mr. Cameron's father has agreed to pay two hundred dollars for father's model! "

" Has he, really? " asked Mrs. Carter, her face lighting up.

" He has bought it, that is, half of it; but he is to pay more than that."

" More than two hundred dollars, Herbert? "

" More than three hundred. What do you think of that? "

" Are you in earnest, Herbert? "

" Quite in earnest, mother; only it is better than a dream. You mustn't be too much excited, mother, when you hear the whole. I will only say that we shan't have to pinch any more, or lie awake thinking how to ward off starvation."

" And can we be together again, Herbert? You don't know how lonely it is without you."

" Poor mother! How lonesome it must have been! Yes; we can be together again, if you think a thousand dollars a year will pay our expenses."

" A thousand dollars a year! " exclaimed Mrs. Carter,

thinking that Herbert was bereft of his senses. "It can't be that your father's invention is worth as much as that?"

"Mr. Cameron has offered that for half the invention, and I have agreed to sell to him. I supposed you would not object."

"Object? I did not dream of getting one-tenth as much. It seems to me like a dream."

"It is a happy dream, mother, and a true one. Father little thought what a handsome legacy he was leaving us when he left us that model."

"How happy it would have made him had he known it before he died! Tell me how it all happened."

So Herbert had to tell his mother about his fortunate meeting with Mr. Cameron, and what resulted from it.

"Mr. Cameron is a very honorable man," he concluded, "for he might easily have offered one-quarter as much, and I should have agreed to it. Now, mother, let me tell you my plans for the future. In the first place, are you willing to leave Wrayburn?"

"I am willing to live anywhere if we are together."

"Mr. Cameron proposed to me to accept a clerkship in his office, but for the present, I told him, I wished to make up the deficiencies in my education. In the town where he lives there is a flourishing academy. I propose that we move there, and I spend the next two years in study. We shall have a competent income, more than enough to support us, and so I can afford the time."

"I fully approve of your proposal, Herbert. We may sometime lose our money, but a good education never."

"I was sure you would agree with me."

"Shall we have any difficulty in finding a house of suitable size?"

"I inquired about that. There is a very pretty cottage just vacated, not far from the academy. I find we can have it at a moderate rent. I have already got the refusal of it, and will write at once that we will hire it."

Herbert's Return

"And what shall we do with this house?"

"We won't sell it to Squire Leech at a sacrifice. That is one thing certain. By the way, day after to-morrow is the day for paying the interest."

"Yes; I have been troubling myself about it."

"There is no occasion; I have a hundred dollars in my pocket, given me on account by Mr. Cameron. So the squire is checkmated. But, mother, I have a favor to ask of you."

"What is that?"

"For two days keep secret our good fortune."

"Why, Herbert?"

"I want the squire to be deceived—to think the place is in his grasp, and realize that there is many a slip between the cup and the lip."

"What shall I say to the neighbors if they ask why you have got home?"

"Say that I am not going back to New York—that I couldn't earn enough there to save anything."

"I will do as you think best, Herbert; but I am afraid that my joy at the good news you have brought will betray me."

"It will be attributed to your joy in having me back. We'll keep things secret for a day or two—that's all."

After supper Herbert walked out. He was popular in the village, and received many cordial greetings. To the inevitable inquiries he replied as he had suggested to his mother.

Presently he met James Leech. He smiled to himself as he saw James advancing to meet him, but assumed a sober, downcast look.

"Hello, Carter! Have you got back?" said James.

"Yes."

"Got tired of New York?"

"I should like New York well enough, if I could make enough money there."

"Then you're not going back?" asked James, in a tone of satisfaction.

"Not at present."

"I thought you'd be coming back," said James, in a tone of triumph.

"What made you think so?"

"I knew you couldn't get along there."

"I supported myself while I was there."

"But you didn't make anything over?"

"No."

"Then you might as well be back."

"I don't know. I am not sure of doing that in Wrayburn."

"I don't think I shall stay in Wrayburn long. Father talks of moving to New York," said James, in a burst of confidence. "What do you expect to do here?"

"Do you think your father would give me work?" asked Herbert, demurely.

"I don't know. He might, if you agreed to sell the house."

"We may, if we can get enough for it."

"You'll have to, anyway. You must be very poor."

"We've got a little money."

"Well, I'll mention your case to father. I'm sorry for you, but I knew beforehand you wouldn't succeed in New York."

Herbert smiled quietly as James walked away.

"He'll be astonished when he hears the truth," thought he.

CHAPTER XXXVI

CONCLUSION

JAMES repeated to his father what Herbert had told him, and the squire jumped to the conclusion that Herbert and his mother were in his power, and must accede to his demand. He decided to take advantage of their necessities, and allow only three hundred dollars for the house.

He entered the little house with the air of a proprietor.

"I suppose you know my errand, Mrs. Carter," he said, pompously.

"I believe this is interest day," returned the widow.

"Yes. I presume you have by this time seen the folly of holding on to the place. You can't afford it, and it is best to accept my offer."

"My mother and I have thought it over, and decided to sell," said Herbert.

"I am glad you are so sensible," observed Squire Leech, in a tone of satisfaction. "I will give you three hundred dollars over and above the mortgage."

"You offered us fifty dollars more before."

"Then is not now. You should have accepted my offer when I made it."

"We have no idea of selling at that price," said Herbert. "Our lowest price is six hundred and fifty dollars over and above the mortgage."

"Are you crazy?" ejaculated the squire, angrily.

"No; we have fixed upon that as a fair price," said Herbert, coolly.

"You know you can't get it."

"Then we won't sell."

"Young man, I apprehend you do not understand how the matter stands. You will have to sell."

"Why must we?"

"You can't live on nothing."

"Of course not."

"You have made a failure in New York."

"I made my expenses while I was there."

"Then why didn't you stay?"

"I wanted to do something for mother's support."

"You have altogether too high an idea of your own abilities."

"I hope not, sir."

"You influence your mother to her harm."

"I don't think so, Squire Leech."

"But in this case you must yield. You can't expect me to wait for my money."

"Do you mean the interest?"

"Of course I do."

"We shall not ask you to wait. I am ready to pay it."

The squire stared in discomfiture while Herbert drew out the precise sum needed to pay the interest.

"Where did you get that money?" he inquired, chopfallen.

"Honestly, Squire Leech. Will you give me a receipt?"

The squire did so mechanically.

"I will give you the three hundred and fifty dollars," he said; "but you must accept it to-day, or it is withdrawn."

"Neither to-day nor any other day will it be accepted, Squire Leech," said Herbert, firmly. "If you choose to pay six hundred and fifty, we will sell."

"You must think I am crazy."

"No, sir; it is a fair offer. If you don't want to buy, we will make another offer. We will rent the house for ninety dollars a year. That is the interest on fifteen hundred dollars at six per cent. I believe a man in your employ wishes to live here."

"Where do you propose to live?" asked Squire Leech, in surprise.

"We are going to leave town."

"Have you got a chance to work outside?"

"Yes; but I have declined to. I am going to school for two years—to an academy."

"But how are you going to live all this time?" inquired the squire, in amazement.

"I shall live on my income," answered Herbert, smiling.

"Income! Have you had a legacy?"

"Yes."

"From whom? I thought you only got a trunk of old clothes from your uncle."

"My legacy comes from my father."

"But he died poor."

"He left behind him an invention, half of which we have sold for an income of a thousand dollars a year."

"A thousand a year!" ejaculated the squire.

"Yes. I have sold it to the father of Mr. Cameron, who employed me last summer. You see, there is no occasion for our selling the house."

"You have been very fortunate," said Squire Leech, soberly. "I congratulate you both."

"Thank you," said Herbert, who privately thought their visitor looked excessively annoyed at their good fortune.

"I will see you about the house," he said, as he rose to go.

"Well, the squire congratulated us," said Herbert, after he went away; "but he didn't look happy when he did so. I shouldn't wonder if he accepted our terms, now that he knows we needn't sell."

Herbert proved to be right. Two days later the squire offered six hundred dollars over the mortgage for the place, and it was accepted.

"The place is worth more, mother," he said; "but it will relieve us from care to sell it."

James was even more annoyed than his father when he heard of Herbert's good fortune; but after his first annoyance he showed a disposition to be friendly. It is the way of the world. Nothing makes us sought after like a little good fortune. James felt that, now Herbert was in a position to live without work, he was a gentleman, and to be treated accordingly. Herbert received his overtures politely, but rated them at their real value.

Two years slipped away.

Conclusion

Herbert has finished his course at the academy, and is about to enter the manufactory as an office clerk. Mr. Cameron means to promote him as he merits, and I should not be at all surprised if our young friend eventually became junior partner. He and his mother have bought the house into which they moved, and have done not a little to convert it into a tasteful home. The invention has proved all that Mr. Cameron hoped for it. It has been widely introduced, and Herbert realizes as much from his own half as Mr. Cameron agreed to pay for that which he purchased. So his father's invention has proved to be Herbert Carter's most valuable legacy.

Squire Leech has been unfortunate. Too late he found that Andrew Temple had deceived and defrauded him. All his large property, except a few thousand dollars, has been swept away, and James, disappointed in his lofty hopes, last week applied to Herbert to use his influence to obtain him a situation in Mr. Cameron's establishment. There was no vacancy there, but our hero has found him a place in a dry-goods store in the same town. Whether he will keep it remains to be seen. Times have changed since James looked upon Herbert as far beneath him. Now he is glad to be acknowledged as his companion. If James profits by his altered circumstances, the loss of his father's property may not prove so much of a misfortune after all, for wealth is far from being the greatest earthly good. For our young friend Herbert we may confidently indulge in cheerful anticipations. He has undergone the discipline of poverty and privation, and prosperity is not likely to spoil him. He has done his duty under difficult circumstances, and now he reaps the reward.

THE END

UNCLE WIGGILY SERIES
By
HOWARD R. GARIS

Four titles of these famous books, fifty-two stories in each. Printed from large, clear type on a superior quality of paper. Numerous illustrations and jacket printed in full colors. Bound in cloth.

Price each $1.00 Postpaid

Uncle Wiggily and Alice in Wonderland   *Uncle Wiggily Longears*
Uncle Wiggily and Mother Goose   *Uncle Wiggily's Arabian Nights*

THOSE SMITH BOYS
By
HOWARD R. GARIS

New and complete editions printed from new plates on a superior quality paper. Each book is wrapped in a special jacket printed in colors. Appropriately stamped and handsomely bound in cloth.

Price each 60c Postpaid

Those Smith Boys   *Those Smith Boys on the Diamond*

THE DADDY SERIES
By
HOWARD R. GARIS

Mr. Garis has won the hearts of little folks with his stories. Each is founded on animal lore and is told in simple language. Large, clear text. Special jacket printed in colors. Bound in clothene.

Price each 35c Postpaid

Daddy Takes Us Camping   *Daddy Takes Us Hunting Flowers*
Daddy Takes Us Fishing   *Daddy Takes Us Hunting Birds*
Daddy Takes Us to the Circus   *Daddy Takes Us to the Woods*
Daddy Takes Us Skating   *Daddy Takes Us to the Farm*
Daddy Takes Us Coasting   *Daddy Takes Us to the Garden*

M · A · DONOHUE · & · COMPANY
711 · SOUTH · DEARBORN · STREET · · CHICAGO

Boy Inventors' Series

The author knows these subjects from a practical standpoint. Each book is printed from new plates on a good quality of paper and bound in cloth. Each book wrapped in a jacket printed in colors.

Price 60c each

1.... Boy Inventors' Wireless Triumph
2.... Boy Inventors' and the Vanishing Sun
3.... Boy Inventors' Diving Torpedo Set
4.... Boy Inventors' Flying Ship
5.... Boy Inventors' Electric Ship
6.... Boy Inventors' Radio Telephone

The "How-to-do-it" Books

These books teach the use of tools; how to sharpen them; to design and layout work. Printed from new plates and bound in cloth. Profusely illustrated. Each book is wrapped in a printed jacket.

Price $1.00 each

1.... Carpentry for Boys
2.... Electricity for Boys
3.... Practical Mechanics for Boys

For Sale by all Book-sellers, or sent postpaid on receipt of the above price.

M · A · DONOHUE · & · COMPANY
711 · SOUTH · DEARBORN · STREET · · CHICAGO

ALWAYS *ASK FOR THE* **DONOHUE**
COMPLETE EDITIONS — THE BEST FOR LEAST MONEY

WOODCRAFT
for Boy Scouts and Others

By OWEN JONES *and* MARCUS WOODMAN
With a Message to Boy Scouts by SIR BADEN-POWELL, *Founder of the Boy Scouts' Movement.*

ONE of the essential requirements of the Boy Scout training is a **Knowledge of Woodcraft.** This necessitates a book embracing all the subjects and treating on all the topics that a thorough knowledge of **Woodcraft** implies.

This book thoroughly exhausts the subject. It imparts a comprehensive knowledge of woods from fungus growth to the most stately monarch of the forest; it treats of the habits and lairs of all the feathered and furry inhabitants of the woods. Shows how to trail wild animals; how to identify birds and beasts by their tracks, calls, etc. Tells how to forecast the weather, and in fact treats on every phase of nature with which a Boy Scout or any woodman or lover of nature should be familiar. The authorship guarantees it's authenticity and reliability. Indispensable to "Boy Scouts" and others. Printed from large clear type on superior paper.

Embellished With Over 100 Thumb Nail Illustrations Taken From Life

Bound in Cloth. Stamped with unique and appropriate designs in ink.

Price, **75c**

M. A. DONOHUE & CO.
701-727 S. Dearborn St.   CHICAGO

BOYS BANNER SERIES

A desirable assortment of books for boys, by standard and favorite authors. Each title is complete and unabridged. Printed on a good quality of paper from large, clear type. Beautifully bound in cloth. Each book is wrapped in a special multi-colored jacket.

1. Afloat on the Flood....................Leslie
2. At Whispering Pine Lodge..............Leslie
3. Chums of the Campfire.................Leslie
4. In School and Out......................Optic
5. Jack Winter's Baseball Team..........Overton
6. Jack Winter's Campmates.............Overton
7. Jack Winter's Gridiron Chums........Overton
8. Jack Winter's Iceboat Wonder........Overton
9. Little by Little...........................Optic
10. Motor Boat Boys Mississippi Cruise....Arundel
11. Now or Never ....Optic
12. Phil Bradley's Mountain Boys..........Boone
13. Phil Bradley's Winning Way...........Boone
14. Radio Boys' Cronies.................Whipple
15. Radio Boys Loyalty..................Whipple
16. Rivals of the Trail.....................Leslie
17. Trip Around the Word in a Flying Machine Verne
18. Two years Before the Mast..............Dana

For Sale by all Book-sellers, or sent postpaid on receipt of 40 cents

M · A · DONOHUE · & · COMPANY
711 · SOUTH · DEARBORN · STREET · · CHICAGO

Motor Boat Boys Series

By Louis Arundel

1. The Motor Club's Cruise Down the Mississippi; or The Dash for Dixie.
2. The Motor Club on the St. Lawrence River; or Adventures Among the Thousand Islands.
3. The Motor Club on the Great Lakes; or Exploring the Mystic Isle of Mackinac.
4. Motor Boat Boys Among the Florida Keys; or The Struggle for the Leadership.
5. Motor Boat Boys Down the Coast; or Through Storm and Stress.
6. Motor Boat Boy's River Chase; or Six Chums Afloat or Ashore.
7. Motor Boat Boys Down the Danube; or Four Chums Abroad

Motor Maid Series

By Katherine Stokes

1. Motor Maids' School Days
2. Motor Maids by Palm and Pine
3. Motor Maids Across the Continent
4. Motor Maids by Rose, Shamrock and Thistle.
5. Motor Maids in Fair Japan
6. Motor Maids at Sunrise Camp

For sale by all booksellers or sent postpaid on receipt of 75c.

M. A. DONOHUE & COMPANY
701-733 S. DEARBORN STREET :: CHICAGO

VICTORY BOY SCOUT SERIES

Stories by a writer who possesses a thorough knowledge of this subject. Handsomely bound in cloth; colored jacket wrapper.

1
The Campfires of the Wolf Patrol

2
Woodcraft; or, How a Patrol Leader Made Good

3
Pathfinder; or, the Missing Tenderfoot

4
Great Hike; or, The Pride of Khaki Troop

5
Endurance Test; or, How Clear Grit Won the Day

6
Under Canvas; or, the Search for the Carteret Ghost

7
Storm-bound; or, a Vacation among the Snow Drifts

8
Afloat; or, Adventures on Watery Trails

9
Tenderfoot Squad; or, Camping at Raccoon Bluff

10
Boy Scouts in an Airship

11
Boy Scout Electricians; or, the Hidden Dynamo

12
Boy Scouts on Open Plains

For Sale by all Book-sellers, or sent postpaid on receipt of 40 cents

M · A · DONOHUE · & · COMPANY
711 · SOUTH · DEARBORN · STREET · · CHICAGO

THE BOYS' ELITE SERIES

12mo, cloth. Price 75c each.

Contains an attractive assortment of books for boys by standard and favorite authors. Printed from large, clear type on a superior quality of paper, bound in a superior quality of binders' cloth, ornamented with illustrated original designs on covers stamped in colors from unique and appropriate dies. Each book wrapped in attractive jacket.

1. Cudjo's Cave .... Trowbridge
2. Green Mountain Boys ....
3. Life of Kit Carson .... Edward L. Ellis
4. Tom Westlake's Golden Luck .... Perry Newberry
5. Tony Keating's Surprises .... Mrs. G. R. Alden (Pansy)
6. Tour of the World in 80 Days .... Jules Verne

THE GIRLS' ELITE SERIES

12mo, cloth. Price 75c each.

Contains an assortment of attractive and desirable books for girls by standard and favorite authors. The books are printed on a good quality of paper in large clear type. Each title is complete and unabridged. Bound in clothene, ornamented on the sides and back with attractive illustrative designs and the title stamped on front and back.

1. Bee and the Butterfly .... Lucy Foster Madison
2. Dixie School Girl .... Gabrielle E. Jackson
3. Girls of Mount Morris .... Amanda Douglas
4. Hope's Messenger .... Gabrielle E. Jackson
5. The Little Aunt .... Marion Ames Taggart
6. A Modern Cinderella .... Amanda Douglas

---

For sale by all Booksellers, or sent postpaid on receipt of 75c

M. A. DONOHUE & COMPANY
711 S. DEARBORN STREET :: **CHICAGO**

KENMORE SERIES
NEW EDITIONS OF FAMOUS BOOKS

THE KENMORE SERIES is composed of select titles by famous authors of boys and girls books. Printed from new plates on a high quality paper. Four illustrations, inlay and wrapper of each book printed in full colors. Cloth-bound and stamped from unique dies.

An Old Fashioned Girl	*Louisa May Alcott*
Black Beauty	*Anna Sewell*
Elsie Dinsmore	*Martha Finley*
Heidi	*Johanna Spyri*
King Arthur	*Retold*
Little Lame Prince	*Miss Mulock*
Little Men	*Louisa May Alcott*
Little Women	*Louisa May Alcott*
Pinocchio	*C. Collodi*
Robin Hood	*Retold*
Storyland Gems for Little Folks	*Winnington*
Treasure Island	*Robert Louis Stevenson*

For sale by all Booksellers, or sent postpaid upon receipt of $1.25

M·A·DONOHUE·&·COMPANY
711 SOUTH DEARBORN STREET · CHICAGO

VICTORY ALGER SERIES

This series contains an attractive assortment of books for boys, by HORATIO ALGER. Printed from new plates on a good quality of paper and bound in cloth. Each wrapped in a printed jacket.

1
A COUSIN'S CONSPIRACY
2
BOB BURTON
3
HARRY VANE
4
HECTOR'S INHERITANCE
5
HERBERT CARTER'S LEGACY
6
JOE'S LUCK
7
JULIUS, THE STREET BOY
8
LUKE WALTON
9
PAUL, THE PEDDLER
10
PHIL, THE FIDDLER
11
RISEN FROM THE RANKS
12
YOUNG SALESMAN

For Sale by all Book-sellers, or sent postpaid on receipt of 40 cents

M · A · DONOHUE · & · COMPANY
711 · SOUTH · DEARBORN · STREET · CHICAGO

The Aeroplane Series

By John Luther Langworthy

1. The Aeroplane Boys; or, The Young Pilots First Air Voyage
2. The Aeroplane Boys on the Wing; or, Aeroplane Chums in the Tropics
3. The Aeroplane Boys Among the Clouds; or, Young Aviators in a Wreck
4. The Aeroplane Boys' Flights; or, A Hydroplane Round-up
5. The Aeroplane Boys on a Cattle Ranch

The Girl Aviator Series

By Margaret Burnham

Just the type of books that delight and fascinate the wide awake Girls of the present day who are between the ages of eight and fourteen years. The great author of these books regards them as the best products of her pen. Printed from large clear type on a superior quality of paper; attractive multi-color jacket wrapper around each book. Bound in cloth.

1. The Girl Aviators and the Phantom Airship
2. The Girl Aviators on Golden Wings
3. The Girl Aviators' Sky Cruise
4. The Girl Aviators' Motor Butterfly.

For sale by all booksellers or sent postpaid on receipt of 75c.

M. A. DONOHUE & COMPANY
701-733 S. DEARBORN STREET :: CHICAGO

GIRLS BANNER SERIES

A desirable assortment of books for girls, by standard and favorite authors. Each title is complete and unabridged. Printed on a good quality of paper from large, clear type and bound in cloth. Each book is wrapped in a special multi-colored jacket.

1. Alice's Adventures in Wonderland....... *Carroll*
2. Alice Through the Looking Glass .... *Carroll*
3. Campfire Girls on a Long Hike .... *Francis*
4. Daddy's Girl .... *Meade*
5. Dog of Flanders, A .... *Ouida*
6. Elsie Dinsmore .... *Finley*
7. Ethel Hollisters 1st summer as a Campfire Girl *Benson*
8. Ethel Hollisters 2nd summer as a Campfire Girl *Benson*
9. Faith Gartney's Girl hood .... *Whitney*
10. Four Little Mischiefs .... *Mulholland*
11. Polly, A New Fashioned Girl .... *Meade*
12. World of Girls .... *Meade*

For Sale by all Book-sellers, or sent postpaid on receipt of 40 cents

M · A · DONOHUE · & · COMPANY
711 · SOUTH · DEARBORN · STREET · · CHICAGO

FURRY FOLK STORIES
By
JANE FIELDING

A series of life tales of our four-footed friends, as related by the animals. These stories are entertaining and pleasing to the young and old alike. Bound in cloth and illustrated. Colored wrapper.

Price each 50 cents postpaid

1. ... Bear Brownie .... *The Life of a Bear*
2. ... Jackie Hightree ...... *Adventures of a Squirrel*
3. ... Kitty Purrpuss .... *The Memoir of a Cat*
4. ... Master Reynard .... *The History of a Fox*
5. ... Scamp .... *A Dog's Own Story*
6. ... Wee Willie Mousie. *Life from his own Viewpoint*

THE JINGLE BOOK
By
CAROLYN WELLS
Price each 60 cents postpaid

A popular book of Jingles by this well-known writer. A comic illustration on every page. Bound in cloth and beautifully stamped in colors. Each is book wrapped in a jacket printed in colors.

LET'S MAKE BELIEVE STORIES
By
LILIAN T. GARIS

Delightful and fascinating stories; printed from large, clear type on a superior quality of paper, Frontispiece and jacket printed in full colors. Bound in cloth and stamped from appropriate dies.

Price each 50 cents postpaid

1. ... Let's Make Believe We're Keeping House
2. ... Lets Play Circus
3. ... Let's Make Believe We're Soldiers

M · A · DONOHUE · & · COMPANY
711 · SOUTH · DEARBORN · STREET · · CHICAGO

THE
EDWARD S. ELLIS SERIES

STORIES OF THE AMERICAN INDIAN; MYSTERY, ROMANCE AND ADVENTURE

Every red blooded American Boy and Girl will be greatly pleased with these books. They are written by the master writer of such books, EDWARD S. ELLIS. There is mystery, charm and excitement in each volume. All the following titles can be procured at the same place this book was procured, or they will be sent postpaid for 25c per copy or 5 for $1.00.

Astray in the Forest	Boy Hunters in Kentucky
River and Forest	The Daughter of the Chieftain
Lost in the Rockies	Captured by the Indians
Bear Cavern	Princess of the Woods
The Lost River	Wolf Ear: The Indian

Read every one of the above Titles
You will enjoy them

M. A. DONOHUE & COMPANY
Manufacturers and Publishers Since 1861
701-733 SOUTH DEARBORN STREET   CHICAGO

BOY SCOUT SERIES

By

G. HARVEY RALPHSON

Just the type of books that delight and fascinate the wide awake boys of today. Clean, wholesome and interesting; full of mystery and adventure. Each title is complete and unabridged. Printed on a good quality of paper from large, clear type and bound in cloth. Each book is wrapped in a special multi-colored jacket.

1. ... Boy Scouts in Mexico; or, On Guard with Uncle Sam
2. ... Boy Scouts in the Canal Zone; or, the Plot against Uncle Sam
3. ... Boy Scouts in the Philippines; or, the Key to the Treaty Box
4. ... Boy Scouts in the Northwest; or, Fighting Forest Fires
5. ... Boy Scouts in a Motor Boat; or Adventures on Columbia River
6. ... Boy Scouts in an Airship; or, the Warning from the Sky
7. ... Boy Scouts in a Submarine; or, Searching an Ocean Floor
8. ... Boy Scouts on Motorcycles; or, With the Flying Squadron
9. ... Boy Scouts beyond the Arctic Circle; or, the Lost Expedition
10. ... Boy Scout Camera Club; or, the Confessions of a Photograph
11. ... Boy Scout Electricians; or, the Hidden Dynamo
12. ... Boy Scouts in California; or, the Flag on the Cliff
13. ... Boy Scouts on Hudson Bay; or, the Disappearing Fleet
14. ... Boy Scouts in Death Valley; or, the City in the Sky
15. ... Boy Scouts on Open Plains; or, the Roundup not Ordered
16. ... Boy Scouts in Southern Waters; or the Spanish Treasure Chest
17. ... Boy Scouts in Belgium; or, Imperiled in a Trap
18. ... Boy Scouts in the North Sea; or, the Mystery of a Sub
19. ... Boy Scouts Mysterious Signal or Perils of the Black Bear Patrol
20. ... Boy Scouts with the Cossacks; or, a Guilty Secret

For Sale by all Book-sellers, or sent postpaid on receipt of 60 cents

M · A · DONOHUE · & · COMPANY
711 · SOUTH · DEARBORN · STREET · · CHICAGO

Radio Boys Series

1. Radio Boys in the Secret Service; or, Cast Away on an Iceberg ....FRANK HONEYWELL
2. Radio Boys on the Thousand Islands; or, The Yankee Canadian Wireless Trail..FRANK HONEYWELL
3. Radio Boys in the Flying Service; or, Held for Ransom by Mexican Bandits..........J. W. DUFFIELD
4. Radio Boys Under the Sea; or, The Hunt for the Sunken Treasure.................J. W. DUFFIELD
5. Radio Boys Cronies; or, Bill Brown's Radio .... WAYNE WHIPPLE
6. Radio Boys Loyalty; or, Bill Brown Listens In........ .... WAYNE WHIPPLE

Peggy Parson's Series

By Annabel Sharp

A popular and charming series of Girl's books dealing in an interesting and fascinating manner with the the life and adventures of Girlhood so dear to all Girls from eight to fourteen years of age. Printed from large clear type on superior quality paper, multicolor jacket. Bound in cloth.

1. Peggy Parson Hampton Freshman
2. Peggy Parson at Prep School

For sale by all booksellers or sent postpaid on receipt of 75c.

M. A. DONOHUE & COMPANY
701-733 S. DEARBORN STREET :: CHICAGO

CALUMET SERIES
of POPULAR COPYRIGHTS

Apaches of New York .... Alfred Henry Lewis
Arsene Lupin, Gentleman Burglar ... Maurice Leblanc
Battle, The .... Cleveland Moffett
Black Motor Car, The .... Harris Burland
Captain Love .... Theodore Roberts
Cavalier of Virginia, A .... Theodore Roberts
Champion, The .... John Collin Dane
Comrades of Peril .... Randall Parrish
Devil, The .... Van Westrum
Dr. Nicholas Stone .... E. Spence DePue
Devils Own, The .... Randall Parrish
End of the Game, The .... Arthur Hornblow
Every Man His Price .... Max Rittenberg
Garrison's Finish .... W. B. M. Ferguson
Harbor Master, The .... Theodore Roberts
King of the Camorra .... E. Serav
Land of the Frozen Suns .... Bertrand W. Sinclair
Little Grey Girl .... Mary Openshaw
Master of Fortune .... Cutliffe Hyne
New England Folks .... Eugene W. Presbrey
Night Winds Promise .... Varick Vanardy
Red Nights of Paris .... Goron
Return of the Night Wind .... Varick Vanardy
True Detective Stories .... A. L. Drummond
Watch-Dog, The .... Arthur Hornblow

For sale by all booksellers or sent postpaid on receipt of 50c.

M. A. DONOHUE & COMPANY
701-733 S. DEARBORN STREET :: CHICAGO